FARINET'S GOLD

FARINET'S GOLD

by

Charles Ferdinand Ramuz

Translated by

John Weeks

SKOMLIN
House of Memory

SKOMLIN
House of Memory and Imagination
For more information visit *www.skomlin.com*

A SKOMLIN Book
Melbourne, Australia

First published as *Farinet, ou la fausse monnaie*
(Farinet, or The Counterfeit Coins) 1932

First international English edition 2019
Translation copyright © John Weeks 2019
Copyright © Skomlin 2019

ISBN: 978-0-6482521-4-8 *(paperback)*
ISBN: 978-0-6482521-9-1 *(eBook)*

 A catalogue record for this
book is available from the
National Library of Australia

About the translator

Curious names, unusual words and the finer points of grammar have fascinated John Weeks ever since he was little, when he had a pet turtle named Spiro and believed that there existed a verb *misle* (pronounced "mizzle"), of which the past tense was *misled* ("mizzled"). Why, he wondered, did nobody ever use the present tense? Once he was put straight about that, he went on to learn French in school, later adding Russian and Polish as he obtained a bachelor's degree from Amherst College and completed a doctorate in Slavic languages and literatures at the University of California in Berkeley. After spending nine months in Poland on a Fulbright fellowship, he returned to Berkeley to teach a class in beginning Polish, where he met Chris Chinni, his future wife, who had enrolled in the course. They now live in Granby, Connecticut, with two dogs, Nakai and Manitou. Over the years, John has translated numerous documents from Russian and Polish. *Farinet's Gold* is his first published literary translation.

Ramuz's Parable of Freedom

His face appeared, until recently, on the 200-franc Swiss banknote. His most famous fictional hero counterfeited Swiss gold coins and became a Robin Hood-like figure whose historical counterpart is now a tourist draw in the French-speaking region of Switzerland. Yet Charles-Ferdinand Ramuz (1878-1947) is little known outside of his native country; it is only since the turn of this century that his works have begun to appear in English translation (thanks in large part to the efforts of Onesuch Press/Skomlin). Even in the Francophone world, recognition has come to Ramuz only gradually. His novels had to wait until 2005 to attain the ultimate distinction in the French literary world — a Pléiade edition.[1]

My project, then, has been to translate Ramuz's great novel, *Farinet, ou la fausse monnaie (Farinet, or The Counterfeit Coins)* and make it accessible for the first time to English-speaking readers. It is the story of a man who, jealous of his independence, defies the power of the State. Ironically, his rebellion takes the form of producing and circulating counterfeit gold coins that are actually worth more than those minted by the government. For this he is beloved by the inhabitants of the region, who share his deep-rooted distrust of the government and help him at every turn. One of them, Joséphine, falls in love with Farinet, and the conflict between his need to be free and her need to be loved drives the story to a tragic conclusion.

The text presents many challenges to the translator. Where Hugo never met an obscure term he could resist, while Flaubert searched incessantly for *le mot juste* and Céline infused his molten magma of argot with lyricism — Ramuz sticks stubbornly to a lexicon so limited and plain as to seem almost simple-minded at times. Yet the effects he achieves with this pared-down vocabulary are startling and often moving. It is as if Hemingway had hailed from the Swiss Alps, rather than the American Midwest.

---

1 At a recent literary conference in Switzerland, one scholar joked that Ramuz was now being translated... into French! (Personal communication from my Swiss friend, Catherine Sarnau, to whom I am indebted for introducing me to Ramuz's writings.)

INTRODUCTION

While Ramuz has a fondness for piling clauses on top of one
another, complete with embedded parentheses, long dashes and
terminal ellipses, his prose is studded with monosyllables — to an
extent not typical for works of literature in a Romance language.
The intention, I believe, is to reproduce the taciturn manner and
inwardness of his mountain-dwelling villagers. *"On vit petit ici, on
vit pas gros."* "They lead modest lives here; they don't live large."
Even for a translator working in English, a language renowned for
its wealth of expressive monosyllables, it is often hard to match
Ramuz's distilled technique.

In *Farinet*, Ramuz's visual palette consists chiefly of primary
colors: red, green and blue, plus an occasional yellow, supple-
mented with black and white. When he goes so far as to employ
an intermediate tint, it is with clear thematic significance, as is
conspicuously the case with pink in his early novella, *Aline*. In
Farinet, the color gray hints at moral ambiguity, as when Farinet,
"immersed in an *ashen* moonlight, a light, *gray* eider-down of
moonlight," wrestles in his mind with a dilemma whose resolution
will determine the course of the rest of his life.

One feature of the author's style has been controversial, and may
have accounted for the lengthy hesitation of the French literary
world to embrace Ramuz.[2] I refer here to his seemingly cavalier
way with verb tenses. In a single paragraph, even at times within
a single sentence, he can alternate among tenses in a bewilder-
ing fashion. To make matters worse, his use of the pluperfect
frequently renders it indistinguishable in meaning from the past
tense. The problem this creates for the translator is something I
have been wrestling with from the outset. My solution — and it is a
compromise at best — is to preserve the pluperfect where it has its
usual meaning, but to replace it silently with the past tense where
the latter conveys the obvious sense of the passage.

I take a different approach to Ramuz's startling insertion of the
present tense in passages otherwise replete with verbs in the past,
imperfect and pluperfect tenses. While he is clearly making use of
the "historical present" for dramatic effect, the juxtapositions can
be stark, as in this excerpt:

> **Il regarde**. Il **voyait** que la pente raide **commençait** juste sous sa per-
> sonne, tombant là brusquement avec ses vignes culbutées; alors il y
> **avait** dans le bas le large fond plat de la vallée, où un peu plus loin y
> est le Rhône, tandis que tout Sion **était** entre le Rhône et lui. (Emphasis
> added.)

---

2 Catherine Sarnau, personal communication.

He gazes. He **could see** that the steep slope **began** just below him and dropped off abruptly with its tumbled vines. Then, down at the bottom, there **was** the broad, level floor of the valley [and] a little farther off **is** the Rhône, while all of Sion lay between it and him. *(Emphasis added; a slightly different wording appears in the main text.)*

I have retained Ramuz's use of the present tense here and in similar passages, which gives the text rather sharp elbows from the standpoint of the English-speaking reader, who is accustomed to expecting an orderly progression of time in a narrative. It is almost as if Ramuz were writing, not in a Romance language, but a Slavic one, where *aspect*, rather than *tense*, is the prevailing grammatical feature of verbs. Such abrupt juxtapositions of tenses are commonplace in Russian, where delineating the temporal sequence of events is often secondary to highlighting the manner in which a given action is *viewed* (whether it happens instantaneously, is in progress, is completed, is seen as a whole or as a recurring event, etc.). With this device, Ramuz frequently arrests the narrative flow to achieve effects familiar to filmgoers the world over, and it is tempting to speculate about the degree to which he was influenced by the cinema of his day.

If we step back from purely grammatical concerns and view the novel in broader terms, *Farinet* presents a slightly unstable yet fascinating mix of archaic and modernist modes of storytelling. As in fairy tales, the hero is engaged in a kind of quest — for freedom — and is assisted in this endeavor by "helpers," both human and non-human. The aged herbalist Sage is wizard-like in his knowledge of medicinal herbs, and he leads Farinet to the vein of gold. Farinet regards the mountains as *people*, wise teachers from whom he has learned the true meaning of freedom. When he escapes from prison, the moon (personified as female and given a speaking part!) demurely hides behind a cloud to darken the scene and conceal his movements. Later on, an apple tree performs a similar service. His legend is likewise burnished by the roosters of the surrounding area, who relay the story of his exploits from village to village.

More in the modernist line is Ramuz's predilection for jarring, unmediated shifts in the narrative point of view. These shifts create a sometimes disorienting stream-of-consciousness flow akin to the method that William Faulkner made famous in his novels of the same period. (*Farinet* was first published in 1932.) One moment, the story unspools in conventional, omniscient-narrator mode, then, abruptly, it is Farinet himself, or Joséphine, or one of the villagers, whose dramatized consciousness carries the narrative forward. The reader is rarely alerted to these transitions by such formal devices as the use of quotation marks.

Adding to the confusion is Ramuz's telling use of the pronoun *on*, which (as anyone familiar with the French language knows) can stand in for any of the personal pronouns.[3] He takes full advantage of this flexibility to suggest a kind of merging of the viewpoints of all the characters in the story. This serves to reinforce the impression of a set of values, an outlook, a particular place in the world, shared by Farinet and his fellow Valaisans. Unfortunately, the English translator does not have, in his or her armory, a word with the elasticity of meaning exhibited by the French pronoun *on*. Thus, it is necessary to choose among the available alternatives according to the context.

But there is more. Ramuz carries this merger of viewpoints a bold step further, and here things get really sticky. He often switches perspective by employing one of the remaining personal pronouns (e.g., *vous*, *"you"*) in place of the expected one (e.g., *eux*, *"them"*) in a given context. Two examples, among many others, will serve to illustrate this unusual procedure. In Chapter Four, a squad of gendarmes arrives in the café where Joséphine works as a waitress. All of the persons mentioned are presented conventionally in a third-person narrative frame: the sergeant, accompanied by two gendarmes, the village chairman and Crittin, the owner of the café. Joséphine is summoned to appear before them. She enters the room, and the point of view abruptly shifts: *"Elle a été devant **nous**..."* ("She came and stood before **us**.") Then, just as abruptly, the perspective shifts right back to the omniscient, third-person mode. Although, to all appearances, this oscillation of viewpoints is unmotivated, I have preserved the jarring pronoun. Contrariwise, when something similar occurs in Chapter Nine, I have adopted a different approach. Farinet has come to pay a visit to the village councilor, Romailler, at the latter's request. In the middle of their conversation, Romailler calls upstairs to his daughter:

3 I was gratified to learn, months after composing these remarks, that Michelle Bailat-Jones makes precisely the same point regarding Ramuz's prose style in the introduction to her translation of *Beauty on Earth* (Skomlin, 2013).

On a entendu le bruit d'une chaise qu'on déplaçait dans la chambre au-dessus de **vous**, on a entendu un bruit de pas. Ensuite la porte s'est ouverte.

There came the noise of a chair being moved by someone in the room overhead, followed by the sound of footsteps. Then the door opened.

In this instance, I have chosen to recast the sentence so as to make it possible to dispense with the pronoun altogether.

It is my belief that this head-spinning rotation among viewpoints, without the conventional verbal signposts to prepare the reader, is intentional. Like Ramuz's handling of the ambiguous pronoun *on*, his startling use of the "wrong" personal pronoun helps to communicate the "all for one and one for all" character of the microcosm that is the proudly independent Canton of Valais.

In real life, the story of Farinet has come full circle in a light-hearted way. In the Valais, where Ramuz's novel is set and where the historical prototype of his hero carried on his rebellion against the government during the mid-nineteenth century, the local communities have recently begun to issue their own unofficial currency, a form of scrip readily accepted by the local merchants. With conscious irony, the Valaisans have decided that these new notes should be denominated in… *farinets*.

John Weeks
November 25, 2018

And old man Fontana went on saying things in a low voice to the two men who were with him in Mièges at the Café Crittin.

"Yes…"

He nodded his head slowly.

Their names were Ardèvaz and Charrat.

"Yes," continued Fontana, "I'm telling you, his gold is better than the government's. And I say he has the right to make counterfeit money, if it's more real than the real thing. What makes the coins worth anything, is it the pictures on the front, huh? These damsels, these women (naked or not), the crowns, the official seals? Or maybe it's the writing on them? Or the numbers, the numbers the government puts on them? Nobody gives a damn about the writing, right? Or the numbers, either. It wouldn't be the first time the government fooled us about the value and the weight, same way a person would. Just ask those who know what's what. The government says to you, 'This coin was worth that much. Well, now it's worth this much…' It's happened before, and it can happen again. They're less honest than Farinet, the governments are, because when you pay his way, it's according to what's in his coins, whereas when you pay their way it's according to what it says on the front…"

He had begun to talk louder and louder without realizing it, then suddenly he went silent, casting a glance over his left shoulder towards the door.

He had no doubt become afraid that someone had entered without his notice while he was speaking, but when he peered into the smoke he saw no one. True, it was still only five o'clock, not the time when there are a lot of patrons (because instead of that they were in their vineyards, their fields or their vegetable gardens). Hence the drinking room was empty, with its two rows of tables that extended all the way to the window in a kind of fog where you could barely make them out. Reassured, Fontana took two draws on his pipe, his cheeks forming two hollows.

He picked up his glass and drank to their health.

The two other men hadn't said a word. They too smoked their brass-capped pipes; from time to time they nodded their heads.

Their elbows on the table, they kept silent. Without a doubt they were waiting for Fontana to go on with his speech (which indeed wasn't finished); that much was obvious to him. So he cast another wary glance over his shoulder — he was facing the wall, with another wall to his right — then lowered his voice all the same out of an abundance of caution (and even, though he knew that the owner was a reliable man and one devoted to Farinet, in case he might overhear him).

"Now if you say that Farinet's just a youngster, I agree, but who'd he get the secret from, who showed him the hiding places? Old man Sage had some papers. He even showed them to me, and I saw them. They came from Paris — yes, Paris — and from Geneva. Certificates, they call 'em. He'd sent some of his powder there to be assayed. Well, there on the papers it said..."

He paused, then he pronounced the three words well spaced.

"It...was...*that*."

He pauses.

"It was there in these papers, and these gentlemen, you see, they're the folks who know more about these things than we do. They're professionals —scholars, authors of books, philosophers. They said, 'It's pure gold, nothing but pure gold.' They wrote it down. It's on these certificates. And, you see, it's Farinet who has them now… The only difference is, Sage left his gold as powder, while Farinet has turned it into coins, but that's his affair. If they aren't always so well made, it's because he doesn't have the right tools. The raw material's there, though. And I'm telling you it's a fine thing to have under your mattress or under a rock in your garden when the time comes. A thing that doesn't grow old, doesn't rot or spoil, doesn't change color or weight — something fixed when everything else isn't — something not just for today, or yesterday or tomorrow, but for all time, which is as old as the earth and will last just as long… What, are we supposed to have gold right here for the taking, and leave it where it is? Does that make any sense? In the first place, I have some myself — it's no secret. I have a hundred francs' worth. What about you, Ardèvaz?"

Ardèvaz nodded by way of saying that he had some.

"You see? How about you, Charrat?"

Charrat smiled.

"Oh, everybody has some, it's perfectly all right."

"Well, is it just that he's in prison and they're going to leave him there?" said Fontana. "It's thieves we put in prison. *He's* the very opposite of a thief. Just ask the owner…"

He calls out, "Hey, boss!"

"I'm going to ask him if he has some, too, and how much. Because he's the one who has the most. For a long time now, Farinet's been paying for his meals with his coins… Crittin has at least a thousand francs' worth of them…I'll ask him. We're among friends here, among friends and trustworthy folks…Hey, boss! Why doesn't he come?"

They were indeed surprised that Crittin hadn't yet come, as he usually did, to drink a glass with them. Ardèvaz stood up.

Ardèvaz opened the door that led to the passage.

But at that moment the door to the street, at the other end of the passage, swung open and a woman entered. Younger than she looked, with a hat on her head and a suitcase in her hand, she was dressed in black, yet white with dust up to her knees. Seeing Ardèvaz, she stops short...

That day in Mièges — at the foot of the cliffs, a little above of the broad valley of the Rhône, behind the walls of Mièges that glittered in the sun — in this hallway, a woman comes in and sees Ardèvaz, but just then Crittin emerged from his kitchen.

"Ah, it's you... I've been expecting you."

He approached her, then caught sight of Ardèvaz.

"Don't go away... It's Joséphine... You don't remember?... She used to work here, two years ago."

To Joséphine, he said, "Come into the drinking room for a moment...There are some people you know..."

Escorting her inside, he said, "Well, Fontana, do you recognize her? How about you, Charrat?... Joséphine..."

"Ah," said Fontana, "of course."

He held out his hand to her.

"How are you?...So you've come quite a ways, by the looks... Ah, from Sion...Ah!" he said. "And how are things in Sion? ..."

"Just fine."

That's the only thing she said, because then Crittin asked her whether she wanted to go up to her room.

He accompanied her to her room, then came back to the drinking room and said, rather cryptically, "Yes, I've taken her on again...because I think something's going to happen. And soon, but don't say anything about it..."

And Fontana said, "It's Farinet... We were just talking about him..."

But Crittin gave a wink.

4

Indeed, that very night, a little after the cathedral clock chimed its twelve strokes, Farinet made not the slightest noise as he got out of the oak bed-frame fixed to the wall where he slept on a straw mattress.

The warden had made his rounds a moment earlier. Lowering the grate over the peephole in the iron-reinforced door, he had seen Farinet stretched out quietly under his blanket, then had gone off to bed himself.

It was a little after the twelve strokes of midnight when Farinet sat up on his bed.

For a long moment he did not move. He was cautious, sizing up the situation (as he was wont to do in everything). For a long time he kept still, needing to assure himself that all was quiet in the *galleys* (as they called the prison in these parts).

He heard not a sound. All he had to do was throw off his covers.

A little after midnight, he rises and goes barefoot to the loophole pierced in the outer wall, where he hoists himself up level with the window by grasping one of the bars. Then, bracing himself in the stone embrasure like a chimney sweep in his chimney, he set to work.

No one ever quite figured out how he had gotten hold of this metal file, but it was easy to see that he had already made use of it, as the bars were sawn three-quarters of the way through. His file began to cough, or rather to make a noise like the breathing of someone with asthma. It paused from time to time, but all remained quiet in the *galleys*, so the file went back to work.

So it was that the first bar was soon completely sawn through, then the second one. Yet both of them were sturdy, having been forged with a hammer on an anvil in the good old days (when people still knew their way around a forge). Nevertheless, they were now cut both at the top and just above the stonework at the bottom. Farinet had decided to leave as much length to them as possible, so as to have the play needed to bend them. He kept still for a moment to let the drumming of his heart subside. With his tongue he lapped the salty sweat from the corners of his lips. It streamed down the back of his neck and glued his shirt to his skin. Now he was sliced at the waist by the light of the moon; it illuminated the lower half of his body, which was like ice, whereas his hands and his head seemed to be on fire. That doesn't matter — I'll show them who I am! He waited patiently as long as necessary, listening with one ear for any sounds coming from inside the prison, and with the other for those that might come from outside. But there was just a horse coughing out there, on the other side of the courtyard wall, then the cathedral clock that chimed one o'clock in the morning. He suspends himself with both hands from one of the bars and lets himself fall back...

"Ha! They thought they had me!" The bar yielded under his weight. "Ha! they thought they were going to keep me in their *galleys* for another six months. They didn't know who I am. Neither did the king of Italy, Umberto the First, but he found out." Farinet moved on immediately to the second bar, unaware of the blood trickling down his arm all the way to his armpit. The second bar, too, has just given way. Each of the bars formed a kind of hook bent towards the floor; there was just enough space above them for him to squeeze through — a tiny space, it is true, one where he could only wriggle through lengthwise — but he knew a thing or two about that! He hadn't run up and down the mountains ever since he was a little boy without learning how to take care of himself. Besides, there was freedom waiting for him, so close, coming to him with the moonlight and saying, "You're almost there, Farinet, just one more little effort, that's it..." Then she said, "Now you just have to tie a knot in the rope…That's it… Make two knots. Don't be afraid."[1]

He was not afraid. For it was true that people liked him, and things did, too. Unlike so many prisoners whose stories you read in books, he had no need to cut his bed sheets up into strips. He had a rope, a real one, made of good hemp and just the length he required, that is to say, around eight meters. He was well liked; people took care of him. And he saw that even things felt affection for him, because at the very moment he finished attaching the rope with a double knot to one of the bars, a cloud passed in front of the moon. The *galleys* are at the top of the town, where they rear their high, bare walls; thus Farinet would have been easily spotted — a dark figure thrashing about against the bright façade — if there had been any moonlight, but there was none. The moon said, "I don't want to hinder you," as she retreated behind a big, black cloud. He lowered himself along the wall into a profound darkness from which he was indistinguishable. He merely had to entrust himself to the rope to its very end and he would reach the ground. His mind was now blank; everything happened very fast. It was as if someone made his moves for him. They followed one another in such swift succession that he had no time even to realize what he was doing. When he reached the end of the rope, his feet hit the ground in absolute silence. He was, as it were, at the bottom of a well — the parapet walk, which was not wide, four or five paces to go at most. He stepped across in silence and the deepest of shadows. The moon, above all the bell-towers of Sion and the bishop's palace, said, "I'm hiding myself." Farinet goes on silent feet to the base of the outer wall, which is five or six meters high — but he knows how to handle this. It's just like when he was out searching for gold, or hunting chamois, and he came to the end of a ledge. At that point, there's no way to turn back, no way to continue, and no way down, either — you go out on these ledges the width of two hands, then all of a sudden they peter out to nothing in the void, with cows no bigger than ladybirds that you have between your legs four hundred meters down below. Here he chuckled to himself. Hah! Maybe they think they can stop me with their sorry excuse for masonry, when the Great Mason himself couldn't do a thing. Go and ask the king of Italy, too, King Umberto the First; you know very well what happened when he wanted to keep me under lock and key. He had walls, too — what good did it do him? With his fingertips, he found a crack above his head; with the tips of his toes, he found another crack in the government's wall. He clings as tightly as he can to the stone, with one arm raised. His other arm gropes higher, sets its grip in turn, and the first one joins it. He pulls on them and boosts himself with one knee. Thus he reached the top of the wall while Sion slumbered. He threw his left arm across the wall, and lay down flat on top of it. Done! The king of Italy... Two or three words, always the same ones, sang in his head, while a warm river flowed from his temples to his ears, where it now made a loud, yet pleasant, roar. It was as if someone were shouting "Bravo!" The king of Italy... the king of Italy...

The horse coughed again.

Then the church clock chimed again.

This time it was the treble bell, because the tenor served to chime the hours and the treble to chime the half-hours. Farinet recalled then that his task was still not quite finished.

He went uphill, cutting across the vineyards, then he flopped in the grass beneath an apple tree.

He filled his chest with the air of freedom. He stretches out his hand; he feels the damp grass beneath his hand and through the fabric of his pants. Lifting his head, he caught sight of the stars again, as he could now see the sky in its full extent, and it is good and it is beautiful.

At the outset, he walked swiftly, more ran than walked, as he climbed the rocky slope between the vinestocks, freshly pulled up and covered with shoots, or down in the ditches they dug for layering the vines, which afforded him welcome cover at first. He had no time to think about anything, preoccupied as he was with keeping his convict pants out of sight and conserving his breath, but now there is a branch of the apple tree over his head and another one hanging in front of him and concealing him.

He gazes. He could see that the steep slope began just below him and dropped off abruptly with its tumbled vines. Then, down at the bottom, there was the broad, level floor of the valley with the Rhône a little farther off, while all of Sion lay between him and the river.

The scene emerged little by little (as his eyes adjusted to the total absence of light, which was reassuring to him), as if chiseled from the black rock. This included the heights of Valère and Tourbillon, which were not as high as he was. The church, which was at the top of the former, and the castle, at the top of the latter, were both below him — that is how high he had already ascended. Now he began to laugh, sitting there, and marveled at how an entire town, with a bishop, a government, a castle — two castles — towers, seven or eight churches, a court, judges, a rendered verdict, gendarmes and jailers, had been unable to hold onto him: all these things and persons put together, while he was all alone against all of them. He was alone; they were four or five thousand. But the fact of the matter is, their justice isn't worth a thing — it's injustice. They lead petty lives down there; they lead narrow lives, false lives (all the while, he was still looking down from above). They spend their lives sleeping in beds, while he felt the grass getting all damp beneath his hand, and it was full of flowers beginning to smell fragrant again. Farewell, then, you there down below. To each his own. They're dead for another two hours and I have all the time in the world while they're dead. They wanted to keep me from living, because I have a life all my own...

"Boldly now!" shouted his heart. "Boldly! There's time enough for what comes next, but for now, some sleep, because everything is going well — but that's because I planned well."

He feels his body in the tall grass; he touches his bare feet, his knees, the baggy, striped prison pants, the hemp-cloth prison shirt with bits of bark in it — but underneath it's me, it's me that's underneath.

He lies back. He lies back with his whole body against the good earth; every part of him is touching it. He presses all of himself against it, the back of his skull, the bone in his nape, both shoulders, his thighs, his calves, his heels.

He sees that nothing has stirred yet in the *galleys*.

He also sees that the stars are beginning to grow pale between the branches of the apple tree and out in front where the vault of the sky is beginning to dissolve; contrariwise, the mountains below are growing in number as the night recedes.

He sat up. He is trying to count them. They are breaking through all over, like teeth from the gums, with their peaks that are white, ever whiter, ever more numerous, one in front of the next in a semi-circle — there's one, there's another one, that makes twenty, thirty, a hundred, five hundred, how many altogether? His head is spinning, but he laughs. "It's mine, it's mine again..." He gazes at the things of the earth, reborn to the good life, here, there, farther off, to the right and to the left, everywhere: the blades of grass you can see up close, the rooftops separating from one another, a bell tower — three, four five of them — the Rhône, the highway on the valley floor. It's all mine. And then there are all the mountains above him, while the stars wink out one by one. Then the cock crows, while at the top of the valley, above the white mountains, a kind of pale mist rises into the sky.

He stood up.

He was moving fast. He didn't feel the stones, he didn't feel the prickling of the stubble or the thorns of the bushes.

His only thought was, "Watch out," because he was also looking at the holes through which his knees appeared; he was looking at his pants and their color, for now they had a color, and you could see that they were yellow with a wide black stripe. But the villages are few and far between on these slopes, all too steep, in this country where the land, too poor and too tilted, is cut up into gorges by the mountain streams tumbling down from the top of the range. He knew all the byways and hiding places; he knew each and every one of the houses, each and every one of the hay-lofts — all of the spaces, built or unbuilt, cultivated or not. Besides, he was already almost there.

One last ravine appears. He merely avoided the path that crossed it by means of a bridge. He went a little farther uphill and clambered up onto an embankment to get behind the hedgerow on top of it.

A hundred meters ahead of him there was a house.

The sun had just struck the roof and its slate tiles had begun to shine.

At the same time, a thin plume of blue smoke emerged from the opening of the wide chimney with the raised cap and rose joyously into the gilded air, while a hunting dog was tethered in front of the door with a chain much too big for it.

From behind the hedge, Farinet whistles three times between his fingers. He whistles in a special way three times behind the hedge and the man who had appeared in the doorway suddenly puts down his wooden bucket, turns his head in the direction from which the whistle calls had come, then advances in this direction after shushing the dog, which whined to follow him.

III

A few months earlier, the regional newspapers had been full of him and his story (for that matter, there were only two or three of them, and they came out only once a week).

It was when he was put on trial for making counterfeit coins.

In the papers they had provided the date of his birth; he was twenty-eight years old. He had been born in Bourg-Saint-Pierre, a village situated at the bottom of one of the valleys that branched off to the left from that of the Rhône and then disappeared into the mountains to the south. He was the eldest child, with two brothers and two sisters. The newspapers told the story of how, when he was still quite young (he was no more than fourteen), his father, known far and wide as a smuggler (this was no more than a league from the international frontier) would take him along to roam the mountains. He would give little Maurice a bag to carry, while he hauled a sack full of tobacco on his own back. Hence, according to the story, Maurice Farinet was trained from an early age to defy the laws and the government. At the age of sixteen, they said, he already had his own rifle. And he used it, without a permit. This was because the elder Farinet was not involved only in smuggling. He would say, "What gives the government the right to force us to pay for killing the creatures that are on communal land and so belong to us?" It often happened that he would drink a bit too much, after coming back from one of his trips, in one or another of the cafés along his route. There, seated in front of a liter of *fendant* and filled with the strength of the wine, he'd say, "By what right? That's why I've never paid anything myself..." He would tell his son, "You're not going to pay anything, either... Ever... Swear to it." And Maurice would swear willingly, because he was of the same opinion as his father.

But then, two or three years later, they had found the elder Farinet over by the Leaning Tower at the foot of a rock wall. He was covered in blood, his head and body shattered, after a fall of more than a hundred meters. It was never discovered whether he had been shot (for he had enemies), or had simply slipped on the rocks, despite being keen-eyed and sure-footed and knowing every nook and cranny of the mountains in the region better than anyone. He had gone out alone this time, and they said afterwards (some men who were working a little lower down in the forest) that they had heard several gunshots during the day, but maybe that was old Farinet himself who had fired them. Nobody ever found out. Either way, he left behind a wife and five children.

As a result, it fell to Maurice, the oldest, to go out and earn a living.

He would hire himself out for the season. He would cut wood in the forest during the winter; in the fall, there was the grape harvest down on the plain. In fact, lots of men from the mountains would come down at this time for a month or two to haul the harvest baskets on their backs or press the grapes, which earned them a bit of money. This is how, when he was about to turn twenty, Maurice had come to be employed by one Romailler, who was one of the four councilmen of Mièges.

That is what the newspapers said, among other things. What they didn't say was what Farinet's reasons were for not going back home, once the harvest was done (and he never did go back up there). His father had left no money and little property for his wife and four children (not counting Farinet) to live on. Up there, at times, there would be no work; at other times, no money. His brothers had grown up; they no longer had any need of him. And it so happened that he had made the acquaintance, in Mièges, of an old man named Sage, who busied himself gathering all kinds of herbs and plants in the mountains and selling them to the apothecaries. The elderly Sage was over seventy years old; he needed an assistant.

Old man Sage lived in a small house built on the site of the ancient ramparts, some distance from the village. He had been living there alone for a long time, for he was thought to be a bit of a water-diviner, as well as a healer, and in addition to his plants, he searched for gold. People even maintained that he had found some. There was, it seems, at the top of the range that dominates Mièges on the north side, more than two thousand five hundred meters up, a vein that old Sage had discovered, and eventually he showed it to Farinet. Time passed. Old man Sage, having neither child nor family, said to himself, "He'll take the place of a son. I'll leave him my house and the place where I find my dust." And so Farinet too had begun collecting the dust. But whereas old Sage was content to collect his gold — in the form of a heap of little yellow stones and flakes that he kept, just as they were, locked in a small box — Farinet, for his part, was more creative and had hit on the idea of making plaster molds and buying a blowtorch. And on the old man's death, he began to put his coins into circulation. Close by, in the gorge of the Salenche, there was a beautiful cave, quite dry, that communicated with the cellar of the house. It was here that he set up his workshop so as not to be taken by surprise. People held him in high regard, because they trusted his gold and because he was generous.

However, misfortune struck one time when he had crossed the frontier with a large quantity of coins to dispose of. The misfortune arose from his thinking that it would be easier (since he was carrying a rather large sum) to exchange his coins in Aosta, in Italian territory, on the other side of the Great Saint Bernard Pass.

It was in Aosta that he had gotten caught.

The police had treated him harshly, and the courts still more so. He had been condemned to six years of imprisonment, of which he had served two before managing to escape.

He recalled the harshness and the difficulties of the journey back. For an entire night and an entire day, he had clambered among the rocks and crossed patches of snow, higher than any vegetation, and had found nothing to eat anywhere. He had had to head right up into the mountains, well above the pass, which was guarded and which, with its little lake and the hostel, he eventually could see during the afternoon several hundred meters below him. He would hide in a rocky stretch, then slide and crawl to the next one, while icy water trickled from beneath each slab; his hands and knees were in the water, and wherever there was a depression, it was still full of snow (despite the fact that this was in the middle of the summer). He hadn't eaten anything since the evening before, and nowhere was there anything that could be of help to a hungry man — not a bush, not the smallest berry, not one single thing that the land produced. What sustained him was his reckoning that he would arrive by nightfall at his house, where he could fill his belly and sleep to his heart's content in compensation, and where he would be warm and under a roof (for he was beneath the sky, so close to the clouds that he could have touched them with his hand as they passed by). He saw, on the path beside the lake, two monks in black robes out for a walk and, a bit farther off, the little customs shack with a customs agent no bigger than one's little finger standing in front of it. Uh-oh! Time to hide! Careful now! He continues climbing up his high cliff all the way to the crest of the mountain, a long way from the places people frequented, and made his stomach keep quiet. Thus, hidden one moment, then out in view, then once again disappearing, he had begun to descend, keeping well above the road in the vast desert of many-colored rocks that came first; then vegetation appeared, and finally evening arrived.

He stayed above the village, which lay just below him.

He situated himself so that their house was the first one he should come to. He waited until night fell. He put his hand on his stomach and told it to keep quiet, but he thought to

CHARLES FERDINAND RAMUZ

himself, "It's going to be a while yet." It had gotten dark; he
saw a light appear in the window of the stable. At this point,
he stepped forward; he recognized his brother Antoine. He
called out to him. But he saw Antoine gape with surprise.
Then Antoine said, "Is that you? Where have you come
from?"

"Listen," said Maurice. "Quick, hide me! I'll tell you all about
it later."

And he headed towards the door of the house, but Antoine
said, "Don't go in. Come with me."

He pointed to an old hayloft close by.

His fatigue and weakness were so great that Farinet didn't
argue. He said, "Do you have anything to eat?"

Antoine went to get him something to eat and drink.

When he was settled in the hay, Farinet ate.

"It would be better if you didn't come in," said Antoine. "It's
a busy path, full of gendarmes. You wouldn't be safe. Eat
and get some rest, and then…"

Farinet was eating, which is why he didn't reply…

"Oh, I read about it in the papers," Antoine was saying…
"Have you come from there?…"

He jerked his head towards the other side of the frontier.

"What, you ran away?… Well, then, you'll have to find a
place where you'll be better hidden than here, because
here…"

Farinet was still eating, which is why he said nothing. Then
he fell back on the hay.

All he said was, "And how's Mother?"

"Oh, she hasn't gotten up for a long time now."

"And Apolline?"

"Married."

"And Léonie?"

"Her, too."

"What about Jérôme?"

"He's found work as a servant."

At that point, he understood everything, even though he was already half asleep. Antoine was now master of the house and he intended to stay that way. For he went on, "You understand, we hadn't seen you for ages—how long has it been? Well, a few things have happened…"

"It doesn't matter," said Maurice. "I would have liked to say hello to Mother."

But Antoine said, "You'd better not. It would upset her. And then you'd have to leave right away all the same…"

Farinet was already asleep; he didn't hear what came after that. The next morning, Antoine even had to shake him several times when he brought him some clothes, fresh linen and twenty francs. He changed his clothes and linen, and took the twenty francs.

Ah, he well remembered his return to Bourg-Saint-Pierre after the tough crossing of the mountain range. Now here he was, back in the mountains again, as the day was breaking. Yet perhaps it was better this way, as he told himself, "We would have quarreled. And then he might have reported me to the authorities to get rid of me…"

Only what was he going to do now? There were two solutions. On the one hand, he could return to Mièges where he had his cave and all of his equipment for making the gold, and where he would be well concealed. On the other hand, he could go to Sion, which is a capital, that is to say, a town, which in turn means lots of residents with lots of houses, where he wouldn't be noticed. In Mièges they would know right away that he was there. In Sion, no one would be the wiser, which for the moment seemed preferable (because the Italian government must have already alerted the government of the Canton of Valais). His beard had begun to grow back; he would let it keep on growing. He now had clothes like those worn by the local people; he was from the area and spoke with the local accent... Finally, he made up his mind to go to Sion.

No one recognized him.

Everything went well, except that at the end of three or four days he was out of money. So one evening he left and in less than three hours made the trip from Sion to Mièges, where he intended to retrieve some of the gold coins he had squirreled away, but the whole house was turned upside down, for the place had been searched. He arrived in the middle of the night and left at once, seized with fear, after slipping one of his coins into his wallet and the rest into a leather pouch he wore slung from his neck. He headed back right away, once again making his way laboriously in the dark among the rocks, across the meadows or through the vineyards — far from the roads — so that he got back to Sion at daybreak.

At that hour the cafés were just starting to open up. Hungry and thirsty, he looked for one that was quiet and out of the way. Thus it was that he came to a side street where a sturdy young woman, whom at first he saw only from behind, was removing the shutters from a shop window, above which could be read a sign in yellow letters: *Café de la Croix-Blanche*. She raised her arms and unhooked, one by one, the wooden panels that protected the glass.

"Can I get something to eat and drink?"

"Of course," she said, without turning around. "As you can see, we're open."

He first glanced inside the café to make sure there was no one there other than her, then he went and sat down — taking the extra precaution of turning his back to the door — at the far end of the room, which was narrow and quite long.

The stout woman came back inside.

"Bring me a half-liter of *fendant* with a serving of bread and cheese."

He still hadn't looked at her; as she went away, *she* had looked at *him*. She said nothing, but went to get the wine, a glass, a plate and a knife, then, on another plate, a hunk of bread and a piece of cheese. When she came back, she also set a pot of mustard on the table. She availed herself of every opportunity to steal a glance at him.

Warily, he kept his head down. Since he had not removed his hat, just about all anyone could see of his face was his beard, which was growing back.

He kept silent, as was natural, and let his appetite do the talking for him. He sliced the bread with the knife; he tossed his glass down in one go. He cut his cheese into squares that he brought to his mouth along with a piece of bread. He tilted backward to drink, raising his elbow. Then, wiping his short moustache with his hand, he went back to eating.

Thus, he didn't see that the waitress continued to observe him, while her practiced hands moved on their own in the midst of the wool and the needles, which made a slight clicking noise. She was seated facing him by the counter. This was when he finished eating and raised his head. At the same time, he recognized her. At the same time, he saw that she recognized him.

He said nothing.

He merely rose halfway, his only thought being to vacate the premises. But suddenly realizing that he hadn't paid his bill, he dropped back onto his chair. He had no means of paying other than with one of his coins.

He took out his wallet, then, while pretending to rummage in it and without raising his eyes, he said, "Mademoiselle, could you perhaps give me change for twenty francs?"

She replied, "Oh, I think so, yes."

He put the coin next to him on the table.

He heard her approach and take the coin.

He was afraid that she would examine it first, his coin, but no, she scarcely looked at it. Now she was leaving the drinking room through a door behind the counter.

In his anxiety, the first thing he did was stand up. He thought that he would have time to get to the street before the young woman came back. Then, however, he sat back down, reflecting that to run away like that, leaving his money behind, was as good as making a full confession. All the woman had to do was give a shout and they would be in hot pursuit. All in all, it was better to wait and trust his luck.

Besides, the waitress was already back.

"That comes to one franc seventy..."

Then, putting the coins down one by one before him, she said, "That makes two, three, four, five...plus five, that makes ten...plus five is fifteen, plus five makes twenty... Thank you very much."

Nickel and silver coins, which he counted with a quick glance. Then he said, "That's right." Opening his wallet again, he poured all the coins into it, except for one twenty-centime piece, which he kept between his fingers.

He moved his chair back and rose, saying, "This is for you..."

"Oh, Monsieur Farinet..."

She called him by his name, and he sat back down.

"Oh, Monsieur Farinet, that's not necessary, I was more than pleased already ..."

Her voice low-pitched and somewhat sad, she pushed the twenty centimes back towards him. Then he looked at her.

"Ah!"

She nodded her head. He said, "Ah! How is it?...Do you know? ..."

"Oh, I recognized you all right."

"Me too, I have the feeling I know you."

"Joséphine Pellanda... You don't remember, in Mièges... At Crittin's...I was filling in for someone...It's going on three years ago..."

"Ah," he said. "It's you, I remember you now."

Then he asked her right off, "And do you know? ..."

"Of course," she said, "just like everyone else. Because they talked about you in the papers..."

"In that case," he said, "I have to go."

"But no," she said. "Why? What's your hurry? You're among friends here. Just so you know, that coin of yours — well, I'm keeping it. I've wanted one for a long time..."

At that, an enormous weight was lifted from his chest, as when a man has been caught under a tree trunk and they've come bringing a jack.

"Is that so?"

"Oh, yes. And there's a lot of others like me. Because we know very well that it's gold and that you don't cheat people."

"As for that," he said. "That's the truth."

She was still standing next to him; being seated, he had to raise his head. Now it was her turn to lower her head: a tall woman no longer very young, a bit on the hefty side, wearing a dark gray blouse with a high velvet collar, her face covered in freckles and her hair neatly pulled back.

And it was plain that what she herself said was the exact truth; he was reassured and at the same time flattered. Then (for this was how he was), he went on, "If you'd like another one, one of my coins, that's easy, because I have some right now. I went to get some last night…"

"Oh, she said, "last night!"

And he rummaged around, meanwhile, under his shirt.

"Oh, Monsieur Farinet, I couldn't…"

"Sure you can," he said, "as a memento and because you've been so kind to me…Take it."

He put a second coin on the table.

They were a bit too yellow, his coins, or a bit too bright yellow.

They were less red than the government's coins. But that was just what proved their quality (he said, and people believed him), because the government's coins were an alloy of gold and copper, while his were made of gold and silver.

"Oh, I don't dare…" she said.

"It gives me pleasure to…" he said.

"Well," she said. "Allow me to bring you a bottle…"

"Is that a good idea? … The boss…"

"Oh, he's never here before nine o'clock… And then, even if he did come… I'm pretty sure…"

"Ah!" said Farinet.

"Yes, he knows who you are without having met you. He's often heard people talking about you. He's also one of your friends… Ah, you have them, Monsieur Farinet, friends…"

"But what if some customers came in?"

"I'd let them in."

The coin was still on the table. Joséphine went to get an unopened bottle of wine, the best in the house. She brought two stemmed glasses.

She was shy and self-assured at the same time.

"That beard doesn't suit you."

"What do you care, if it keeps people from recognizing me?"

"It doesn't."

"No, maybe not you, but other people, the gendarmes… And if they put out a description of me…"

"Where are you staying?"

"Nowhere. Up to now, I've stayed in a different place every day."

"Listen, what if you stayed here? There are some rooms in the courtyard."

"The problem is, I don't have any papers."

"That doesn't matter," she said. "You're from these parts, aren't you? And then the boss, well, I'm sure he'll go along… I'll just have to speak to him, of course…"

It was settled that he would come back in the afternoon.

Then, at first, everything was easy for him, too easy, after he escaped from the prisons of Aosta. He was not only protected, but even looked after and spoiled. She was no longer all that young, nor really good-looking, he said to himself, but she had a good heart. So he went along, that is to say, he allowed himself to be spoiled and protected, paying for his lodgings with his coins. With the boss's connivance, he passed himself off as a cousin of Joséphine's.

At first he was cautious, then he was no longer so. For the first few weeks, he didn't show himself in town until after dark. But then, when no one seemed to notice him, he started to go out at any time of day, and even went on two or three occasions as far as Mièges. He told himself that the authorities must have forgotten about him. The result was that, over Joséphine's objections, he twice went out hunting with his friends, which brought him as far as the grape-harvest fair held in Sion, towards the middle of September. There they sell wooden wineglasses, squat larch-wood wine kegs, goatskins with the hair on, veal hides, mule harnesses, and everything else needed for the grape harvest, the pressing and the cellaring. Also on sale, for the young ladies, were brooches, silk scarves and shoes. On the main square where they displayed the livestock just brought down from the mountains, there was a throng of people towards noon; later on, the crowd migrated to the cafés. That was when everything went wrong. Afterward, Farinet acknowledged that he had been partly to blame. After all, he should have known that the police were looking for him.

This was just the time, if ever there was one, to take precautions, what with all the strangers crammed into the Croix-Blanche. But he was emboldened by two months of freedom and things going much too smoothly; concealing himself was the farthest thing from his mind. Farinet appeared at noon at the Croix-Blanche, and took a seat in plain sight at one of the tables, where he ate and drank with his friends Charrat and Ardèvaz.

At the tables nearby there were some people from Mièges who called out to him, "Hey, Farinet! Well, what do you know — it's you! How are you?"

They drank a toast to his health and said, "Here's to you, Farinet!"

They said to him, "What are you doing here? Why don't you come and see us? The door's always open."

And the name, pronounced out loud and even shouted out several times, reverberated all around the café; it was already no longer unknown, even to those who couldn't care less, on account of the items in the newspapers.

It has to be said that Farinet was starting to lose his composure. He kept on drinking at the Croix-Blanche all afternoon (and at one of the tables in the back, just in case he needed to duck out the back). But the gendarmes are well-informed folk. They arrived at the street entrance and in the courtyard at the same time. Suddenly there were two of them at the rear door, and two at the front door. Farinet was thus in the rear of the café, with his back turned to the entrance; but, at a certain moment, it was the other door that opened, and a sergeant appeared, with gold stripes on the black fabric of his sleeves and a revolver in his belt.

He gave a military salute and said, "Nobody move!"

The din of voices and laughter abruptly died down and then ceased altogether.

The sergeant stepped forward, in the profound silence.

Another gendarme, without stripes, appeared in the open doorway behind him.

The sergeant went straight up to Farinet.

"Do you have your papers?"

Farinet stood up.

"I know what this is all about…"

This happened in the middle of September.

IV

It was not until two days after his second escape that the gendarmes showed up in Mièges, evidently because the search was first conducted in the vicinity of Sion, where it was known that he had kept hidden for a long time. From here it is two or three leagues to Sion. Situated on the flank of the mountain, it is a place where there is precious little to eat. The village of Mièges is nothing more than a hamlet. In olden times, it was more of a fortress, of which a few walls and the ruins of some towers were all that remained. Then a street had been laid out within the walls; lining it is a succession of half-ruined and empty houses, still visible to this day. Behind them, on the slope of the mountain, there is only a handful of cottages and a few haylofts forming a lane at a right angle to the street. That is all there is. It is a wretched place. The lowlands are too marshy to produce anything but a bit of bad hay to be used as bedding. There is hardly a thing to keep a soul alive, aside from the vines (which are good) and the pastures up on high; there are few people about, eking out a mean existence. As a result, the village contains hardly more than two hundred inhabitants, which is to say far fewer than in times past. Here it is as if you stood at an observation post, with the mountain at your back, a gorge to the east, a wall with a door to the west, and the empty expanse of the plain in front of you.

The gendarmes could be seen coming from a distance, that morning two days later.

Us, we pretended not to notice. We saw them stop a woman on the road in the middle of the plain, but she must have been playing dumb too, because she shook her head.

They came and approached old man Bruchet, who was warming himself in the sun in front of his house.

It was a big blue, two-storied house, which happened to be one of those still barely standing. In the façade, there was a large crack running diagonally from a sundial all the way to the roof. With his cane between his legs and his head thrust forward beneath his rust-colored hat, old man Bruchet heard the sergeant out, seemingly without understanding a word, then twice shrugged his shoulders.

His aged, gray hands, covered all over with ink spots like blotting paper that has long been in use, did not stir from their position. On one of the windowsills there were carnations in a chamber pot filled with dirt.

The gendarmes went up the lane. One could have thought now that the village had been abandoned. There was not a person in sight anywhere. A few women, who appeared momentarily in their doorway or on the front steps, rushed back inside. The children were in school and the men must have been in the vineyards or out in the fields. The gendarmes went to see the mayor, who turned out to be away from home as well. They had to go in search of him, while the little curtains in the windows of the neighboring houses were raised one after another.

The mayor had a lengthy conversation with the sergeant. He then accompanied the gendarmes to Farinet's house.

It stood outside the village, to the east. The four men had to walk quite some time among fallen rocks fenced off by low walls, behind which a few muscat vines had been planted. Farther to the right, on the brink of the gorge, a tower broken slantwise called to mind an old tooth.

Here it was, among the stones. The house itself was scarcely more than a heap of stones beneath a roof made of fat slabs of rock; it was just visible from the midst of a tangle of branches.

Apparently, the search produced nothing, because it didn't last long. The four men came back. The mayor did his utmost to appear obliging, for he stayed with the gendarmes and spent the whole morning with them.

The four of them came back down the lane, then all four were seen heading for Crittin's café. The two or three customers in the drinking room had managed to slip away in time through the door to the gardens out back.

Thus, the only one left to greet them was the owner, a fat man whose sack of a belly made his shirt bulge. In spite of his leather belt, his pants would not stay put. He kept pulling them up. He went to greet the gendarmes in the entry, and seemed none too surprised by their presence. All the while tugging on his pockets to pull up his pants, he said, "No...no, I haven't seen him...I don't know anything..."

He seemed perfectly assured, perfectly at ease.

"Wouldn't you like to sit down, sirs? What could I bring you?"

However, the sergeant appeared not to have heard him. He was not from the area, nor were the two gendarmes. They had been sent from Sierre (as came to light later on); the barracks in Sierre are at the other end of the valley.

They remained standing, as did the café owner, and the mayor likewise. It was at this point that the sergeant drew from his tunic some papers bearing an official seal. Taking off his *képi* and setting it on the table, he unfolded one of the sheets, which was an arrest warrant.

The owner kept shaking his head.

"But you do know him well?"

"Yes," said Crittin, "but we haven't seen him for a long time."

They couldn't get anything else out of him.

"That's not all," the sergeant went on to say.

He looked Crittin in the eye.

"You wouldn't happen to know a woman by the name of..."

He seemed to be having trouble making out the name, then he came out sharply with, "Joséphine Pellanda?"

"Yes," said the owner.

"Aha!" said the sergeant. "Where is she?"

"Here," said the owner.

The whole time he appeared not the least bit perturbed or anxious; his manner was as natural as could be, like that of someone who merely has to tell the truth and nothing but the truth. The sergeant went on to ask him, "Here? What is she doing here? …"

"She's my waitress," said the owner.

"Your waitress? Since when?"

"Let's see…" said Crittin… "For the past…three years, three and a half years…"

"In that case, what was she doing in Sion these past few days? …"

"She'd gone to see her mother."

"How long did she stay at her mother's place? …"

"Five or six months," said the owner.

He spoke without the slightest hesitation, because as a matter of fact he was only telling the truth, and the truth is always easy to tell. So, when this next question came his way, he again said nothing that was not strictly true, if you will.

"And when did she come back?"

"The day before yesterday."

"At what time?"

"Around five o'clock."

"Ah," said the sergeant. "Can I see her?"

"Of course. I'll go and get her for you…"

Meanwhile, the two gendarmes decided to sit down. They too removed their *képis*, placing them upside down on one of the tables so that the red lining made of imitation silk was exposed to view.

29

The mayor sat down in turn. The sergeant remained standing, holding his papers in one hand and mopping his brow with the other. No one said another word.

A clock creaked, over and over again, each time the brass bob of the pendulum passed behind the round pane. The walls were painted in tempera, but the blue color had worn away from being rubbed by heads and shoulders just above the benches, and all around the room there were spots in the form of white bands beneath two or three posters or framed paintings.

Some of these were unframed and crudely mounted with nails driven into all four corners.

They heard the owner's footsteps receding, then they heard nothing at all but the clock. Some time passed. Then the sound of footsteps could again be heard, coming back in the stairway and approaching rapidly. At that, the sergeant put his handkerchief back in his pocket. Josephine came in, while behind her the owner shut the door with care.

She came and stood before us. She did not say hello to anyone (nor did anyone say hello to her); she then waited with her hands clasped in front of her apron.

Everything was done in a very official manner. The sergeant looks at her; glances at his papers; looks at her again more closely from head to foot, each time consulting the sheet where there were handwritten items next to printed ones.

"Is your name Pellanda, Joséphine?"

"Yes."

"Born in Sion. In the year—?"

"Yes…"

"On March 24th?"

"Yes."

"Unmarried? …"

He looks at her.

"Yes."

He consulted his papers again.

"Your occupation?"

"Waitress."

"You are employed here?"

"Yes."

"For how long?"

"Three years last Easter."

"Have you ever been away from your job?"

"Yes, often."

"Why?"

He looks at her. She has been looking at him continuously; she hasn't taken her eyes off him, eyes black and small, set in a broad, dark-complexioned, innocent face. Their expression was unchanged; they displayed all at once a good deal of composure, pity, patience — and defiance withal.

"Because my mother's in Sion. And because she's old and sick a lot." (This was true, but she lived with another daughter who was married and able to take care of her.) "So," said Joséphine, "she needs me."

"When was the last time you were there?"

"Last week."

"So you have been back for four days already?"

"No, I came back the day before yesterday."

"At what time?"

"At five o'clock."

"Where is your room?"

The sergeant said to the owner, "We're going to have a look there."

The bench the gendarmes were sitting on fell over with a clatter, as the two of them jumped to their feet. The owner led the way, followed by Joséphine and the sergeant, with the mayor and the two gendarmes bringing up the rear.

It was a shabby attic room, the walls lacking wallpaper and revealing plaster full of scratches and dotted with black fly specks. A small iron bed, a deal table and a rush chair constituted all there was in the way of furniture.

The sergeant, without saying a word, approached the bed. He uncovered it, removing the blanket and the sheets, then he turned over the pillows and the mattress. He had his men drag the bed to the middle of the room to make doubly sure that there was nothing hidden beneath it.

He opened the wardrobe; it was empty.

There remained a suitcase, bound in red canvas, lying open in a corner. He tossed the contents onto the table.

They consisted of women's garments.

The sergeant picked up the articles of underwear and clothing one by one and handed them to his men, who shook them so as to make anything that might have been concealed there fall out: a blouse of coarse fabric with half-length sleeves, another blouse, two or three pairs of hand-knitted stockings, a skirt, a black caraco, some scarves and a few handkerchiefs.

She lowered her head slightly now and kept silent, as did the owner, the mayor and the gendarmes.

"You don't have any of the money? ...You don't have any... any of the coins. The fact is, you've been reported. Show me your pockets."

Suddenly, Joséphine's eyes flashed, yet she maintained her composure. She made a slight movement to one side, holding her hands as far away as possible from the sergeant's, then she gave in…

"You better watch out," said the sergeant, "because we're going to keep an eye on you… Can it be possible that you don't know him?…You don't know what it's all about?… No?… You haven't by any chance heard someone mention the name Farinet? … Farinet, Maurice…"

"Yes," she blurted out.

He had just moved away. For her part, she had drawn herself up straight.

"Oh, yes," she said. "I know him well, I know him better than you do…"

She burst out laughing as the sergeant and the two men were going out the door.

"And I know very well that he's escaped. Too bad for you, but so much the better for him, and so much the better for us, because we like him…Everyone likes him here."

Her voice pursued the sergeant down the stairs.

"Isn't that so, Mister Mayor?… And what about you, boss, what do you think?…"

Then her laughter rang out again, but the sergeant and his two men were already out in the street and soon gone from there as well; meanwhile, people appeared as if by magic and gathered there.

"Well?" said one.

"Well, naturally, they didn't find a thing."

That brought a laugh.

"And, naturally, since they didn't find anything, they couldn't arrest anybody, so they went away empty-handed."

More laughter.

"Where are they going?"

"Oh," said one, "they're going to continue with their tour."

And he raised his arm in the direction of the mountain, which wasn't visible on account of the houses.

"They're bound to go up to the chalet, because they know full well that he keeps his gold up there."[2]

"In this heat!"

"And dressed the way they are! You know how thick those uniforms are, plus they're black and have collars. And that's not counting the load the fellows are carrying, what with the cartridge belt, the rifle, the knapsack, the bayonet…"

"What do you expect? That's their job."

"What if they find him up there?"

"Not a chance."

It was funny how, with the telescope, he couldn't see anything at first from up there, except a white disc speckled with tiny black dots.

A luminous disc, in which there was nothing but the light, a disc of light devoid of objects. It took a long time to slide the brass tubes inside one another until they (the objects) finally appeared, vague and ill-defined at first, like a mist, a bit of fog, blue, gray or green — then clearer and clearer, as Félicien, while keeping his eye glued to the small opening, managed to adjust the telescope, which was almost two feet long, to the right length.

He kept sliding the tubes together, one inside the other, just for the fun of making them perform their trick of destroying the world and putting it back together again.

He had been there since noon, on the lookout for the gendarmes. It was a kind of balcony. When Farinet had arrived the morning of the day before, the master dairyman had immediately said to his two sons, "Take the telescope." And from that moment on, they had worked in shifts here, where the pasture came to a point jutting over the void, like the prow of a ship whose deck was painted green, in the middle of the air.

Directly beneath him, but fifteen hundred meters lower down, he could see Mièges, which seemed to have slid down bit by bit and come to rest clinging, along with its handful of old houses, its ruined towers and its ramparts, to the slope of the enormous scree field. But here everything slides, or has slid at one time, on these thin layers of schist that cover one another like sheets of tin. The land is given to sliding here; the rocks, the boulders, the stones right down to the fine gravel are caught up in it. The whole mountain drops down its length as it erodes and wears away, shattered by the freezes and polished by them more and more from one day to the next. It is as if there were immense tents everywhere (some of them three thousand meters high), their canvas perfectly taut in a uniform slope all the way to the ground. Here and there, a few swellings would persist (as when the canvas dries out after getting soaked), along with a few traces of wrinkles, more than half-erased; meanwhile, the tents shine dazzlingly overhead. Only on the ledges were there scraps of organic soil, in the cracks and crevices, and in certain hollows not yet completely worn down. Here there were patches of green and a few bushes; there a bit of grass was visible, or, lower down, some vineyards. But elsewhere the land was entirely bare, with the result that there was nothing to conceal the path's tightly packed twists and turns, blasted through the rock with dozens and hundreds of mines, from the village all the way up here. "Just go where I told you," the master had said to his boys, then, turning to Farinet, he said, "As for you, I guarantee that you'll be able to sleep undisturbed."

The two boys had taken the telescope and begun to keep watch by the light of the moon. When they looked at the moon through the telescope, they were amazed by her mouth and her eyes. But the countryside down below was even more fun to look at, now that it was Félicien's turn and the afternoon had begun.

At first, he had been unable to make out a thing. It was just a disc of light sprinkled with dark specks, as when you look at a sheet of paper with a magnifying glass. Then, all of a sudden, between the rocks on a patch of grass, there were life-sized flowers in a spot where water oozed out, leaving a dark stain on the white schist.

He put down the telescope, which he had been holding in front of his right eye with the other one closed. How far could he see with the naked eye?

The pretty mountain flowers, with their dazzling colors, bluer than blue, whiter than white (the crocuses, the little gentian), more yellow than yellow, like the flower of the mountain arnica — but he had already forgotten about them, because a cloud was passing by, and he aimed at the cloud.

Once again, he aimed at the plain. He dropped down 1,500 meters, which is just a slight movement to make with the big end of the telescope.

He saw a dry-stone dike between tufts of reeds growing in very fine sand, smooth as porcelain.

The swiftly flowing water raised short waves with sharp crests that overtook one another, white like wine that has just fermented. This was the Rhône.

It was high, in this season of melting snows, and much enlarged. When he aimed the telescope towards the middle, it appeared to have no banks: it escaped its bounds as if the entire plain had been overspread by its floodwaters.

It was as if the whole valley floor were itself in motion and descending with this deluge; meanwhile an ancient little church with a six-sided bell tower also came into view, along with its yellow tiles, its steeple and the road. A small child in shirtsleeves was nibbling a large hunk of bread...

All of a sudden, Félicien remembered the gendarmes.

He had to tilt the telescope down and bring it closer to his body, so that he was holding it practically against his body and looking between his knees.

From bend to bend in the path, Félicien carefully went up the slope and then back down from bend to bend. Thus it was, towards two o'clock, that these three black dots suddenly stood out next to the little muscat vineyard by the tower, as they emerged from behind an embankment.

Félicien had to go only a few steps, and cup his hands to his mouth, in order to warn those back at the chalet.

He saw his father come out, then three of his men. They came running, to have a good laugh, with his father in his thick beard leading the way.

They saw the three black dots, then they couldn't see them anymore.

They saw them again.

The five men had sprawled on their stomachs and were passing the telescope back and forth.

§

The gendarmes did not arrive until late in the afternoon. The master was lighting the fire. The men in the pasture were busy gathering the herd. As they did every evening, they raised their whips and called out to the animals in the pasture — and the latter come or dawdle, in groups or singly; they form brown dots in the grass, which is still as thick and sweet as it was at the beginning of summer, beneath the towering white rocks; some of the younger ones, seized by a mad whim, take off at a gallop jingling their bells and have to be chased — "Ho, there!"

It was at this moment that the gendarmes made their appearance. Those in the chalet affected to be greatly surprised to see them.

The master was the first to look quite surprised, as he went to the front step.

He said hello to them from the midst of his thick beard, but he had to raise his voice on account of the jingling cowbells, which together filled the air with a din like that of a waterfall.

The sergeant came to a halt. He and the master began a conversation.

The sergeant stood on the doorstep, with the gendarmes a few paces away from him. Behind the master, the fire in the hearth stirred, a study in red like a bouquet ruffled by the wind, against the black of the wall glazed with soot.

The master is calm within his beard. The sergeant — flushed red beneath his *képi*, his moustache drooping, the collar of his tunic unhooked and the three top buttons likewise unfastened over his shirt — is white with dust like his men. And the master says, "Of course, we've seen him, but you've arrived too late…"

He laughed.

"Surely you don't think he'll let himself get caught like this, do you?"

And gesturing towards the rocks, he said, "There's no end of space around here, or trails, or passes, or hideouts…Who knows but what he isn't already over on the German side?"

The herd was coming in and being driven into the pen. The two men could barely hear each other, hence the master had to raise his voice still louder.

"But come on in anyway…Have a bite to eat."

The sergeant did not refuse, nor did his men. They were not about to stand on ceremony, having been on the road since early this morning. Besides, up here they were beyond any supervision and so far away from the settled areas that it was as if their official mission was over.

While the milking commenced in the cow pen, the gendarmes reverted to being men like any others — seated at the big table, they were just hungry and thirsty, and happy to sit awhile in the shade before a liter of cool wine, the round loaf of black bread and a wedge of aged cheese.

"It's yesterday morning," the master was saying, "yesterday, bright and early..."

He clinked glasses with them, then, standing before them with his glass in his hand, he said, "We saw him with the telescope...Yes, on the other side of the gorge. Now someone who knows the country the way he does, a mountaineer like him, a hunter like him..."

He laughed into his beard,[3] not too much, not showing it too much, as he turned, with his beard, towards the sergeant.

"...and one who doesn't hunt anything but the chamois," he said, "or so it seems. And it also seems as though they had no idea how to keep him locked up in Sion. I have to think the lodgings weren't to his liking. There must not have been enough air and room for him. Because this is a fellow used to having room, lots of room..."

He laughed.

"...To your health!"

Then he went over and tossed a couple of thick larch branches onto the hearth. They were as twisted and knotty as vinestock, with good-smelling, pink bark and fat, white pearls of resin on their scales.

The sergeant said nothing in reply. He seemed totally absorbed in drinking and eating, as did his men. They ate and drank some more, then lit cigars.

They brought in the milk in wooden pails: fine, white, frothy milk that—when poured from above into the copper boiler—spread out as it fell to form a flat skin, as thin as a sheet of linen.

The sergeant spoke up.

"Well, we have to be on our way. Thank you very much…"

They said nothing more about Farinet. As for him — he hadn't let them out of his sight.

And just as the gendarmes were about to leave the pasture, they heard this loud cough — it was the mountain that coughed.

They had to crane their necks way back. They had to direct their gaze above the chalet, above the rock wall (which was beginning to turn pink) that towered over it, then higher still and farther back, up the grand façades like pale white cloth stretched taut all the way to the sky.

Up there, there was a puff of white vapor. Up there, there was something like a tiny white column. It was there already, but they hadn't seen it before the explosion; it was still there after the explosion came and forced them to look.

It was there, slowly rising, the tip bending and widening into a cap shaped liked a mushroom. Little by little, it too took on a pink coloration.

It was Farinet, setting off one of his explosive charges by way of a sendoff to the gendarmes, just as they were about to go out of sight.

For the silence was broken anew, and three times the gorges and the rock walls shouted in the distance, "Hurrah! Hurrah! Hurrah! …"

V

He had gone straight back up to his lode.

Scarcely had he broken out of the *galleys* than he was once again on his back, in his pit at the top of the range, making the case against him worse still. Here, he first split the rock with a pickaxe, the way those who mine coal do. Now he was working with a chisel like a sculptor, while the water fell drop by drop from his face.

He was three or four meters deep inside a gallery just wide enough to let his body pass through. Here, with both shoulders touching the floor, he worked with his arms raised, while one drop fell, then another and another, from the rock face, and they merged with the sweat on his lips and were just as salty — but so what?

Was not freedom his?

He emerged from his pit. He sat on the ledge. He settled himself against the rock wall. First he made sure he was snug against it with his whole body, as if he were afraid of being swept off. Then there was nothing else to do but let his gaze wander, for whichever way he turned, there was nothing but the void.

He had to lean forward a bit to see the chalet in the pasture, right between his knees. The cows, brown and black, were scattered dots that he had to stare at for a moment before seeing them move, the size of ladybirds, while at the corner of the roof the blue smoke stands erect like a jay feather. The rock all around him shines in the sun like an angel's wing, in which the gold and silver are combined. He was close to three thousand meters up (that is, where all grass ends and only a few mosses still manage to survive), suspended in the air as if on a flying machine, with nothing in front of him and at the same height but the air. In front of him, there was nothing but air. Then, letting his gaze drop still more, he saw this air actually turn blue as it thickened, because off in the distance the wide valley of the Rhône opened up — indeed, this is one of its widest stretches, with its sandy bottomland where they grow asparagus and apricots. And once again, in front of him, there was nothing but air. Then, beyond this veil, as when one looks through a window of colored glass, there were, arranged in a semi-circle stretching to infinity — both to his right and to his left — the high peaks of the Alps of Valais, then those of Savoy, then even those of Dauphiné, seated together and praising God.

All was going well; he had found some gold. Sometimes he labored for entire days without finding any; other times, after an hour or two, he already had enough dust to fill one of the two leather pouches fastened to his belt. He would say to himself, "You've done your day's work, you can take a rest." To get out of the ore pit, he had to crawl on his back using the palms of his hands and his heels, but once he reached the open air, he just had to hunch the upper half of his body forward in order to sit up. He was in full sunlight. He opened his pouch. He let the contents trickle between his fingers.

It's liquid, fine, soft and pleasing to the touch; it's nice to caress, like a woman's hair!

He let the dust flow from one hand into the other; it glittered in the sunlight. It isn't gold yet, he thought, so long as it is hidden in the earth. It needs to come out into the light for it to awaken and catch fire, because it is a kind of sun and it recognizes its kinship. But take a look at it now: it has a rich color, like that of *fendant* in a good year. It's soft, it's tender and fine. And what's more — it's freedom (he looked around him, and freedom sang to him in his heart). If only they'd come and see how good it is to be here, better than in their offices, better than in their prisons, better than in their streets. But they couldn't come, even if they wanted to — it's too high up and exposed for them, these judges, because they're old, or for these government officials, who are all knotted up with rheumatism, or for these overfed gendarmes... I'd say to them, "Well, is it gold or isn't it? You can see where I found it. It's the mountain that gives it to me. The mountain is freedom... And what difference does it make now whether you believe me or not? ..."

He held out his pouch, wide open, so that this gentle fire was in the light. Then, raising his head, he inhaled the air, which was hot and cold at the same time. He looked around him and saw that he was alone up in the air, and all of a sudden — this sprang from his heart — he said to himself, "Freedom..."

But what is freedom?

It's when you do what you want, the way you want to, and when you feel like it.

It's when you depend on no one but yourself. It's when all the commandments spring from you. You want to stay in bed, stay in bed. You want to get up, get up. You want to eat, well, go ahead and eat. You don't feel like eating, then don't eat... And if you want to coin money, you can coin money...

He began to laugh.

He closed his pouch and double-checked to make sure it was tied fast to his belt, then pulled his shirt down over it. He went to take a drink from the little wooden wine-cask (which he kept cool in a fissure beneath the overhanging cliff). Then, having finished his drink, he turned around and, just like that, he was struck yet again by all the beauty of the world and all the grandeur of the world.

He staggered like a man drunk; he stepped back and put his hand over his eyes.

Then, little by little moving it away, he began to gaze at all of these things — so often seen and yet, as it were, never seen before; reborn each time from nothing; revived from death even; raised up before him in all their newness — so that each time he had to orient himself anew, due to the changes in the cloudy or cloudless sky, the changes in the air and the lighting, as well as the changes that took place within him.

He was sitting on the brink of the ledge, so far forward that his legs dangled in the void.

Here he leaned forward a little, and the first thing he made out between his knees was the chalet (its roof covered with slate shingles), set down flat amidst the greenery next to a glistening round pond. The pond was the size of a watch crystal, the roof no bigger than a missal whose black binding is turning gray from wear.

From time to time, there rose a shout from down in the pasture or the pealing of a bell. Then he would laugh at the sight of the cows no bigger than squash seeds, while the men were just specks like radish seeds.

Then, casting his gaze farther out, he dropped down another level, then dropped again, straight down, fifteen hundred meters or more, all the way to the Rhône, which had become something like a thin, white cord in a sort of soapy water — the air. From there, he went back up the opposite slopes, through the gorges and valleys, onto the round tops covered with green woods, then with black woods, then with meadows together with villages; next there came a first rock wall, then some pastures, then still more rocks, then…

And, first, he had to close his eyes again. First, he had to get them used to this view again.

In morning light (as on that day) and at an early hour, with the sunlight coming at a low angle, it was like a blaze of wood shavings.

By lifting his gaze high enough, to where he now directed it, he was on the verge of catching fire from these embers and these firebrands. From the farthest point to the east (the Canton of Bern or the Canton of Uri) to the extreme west (the middle of Savoy or farther still), for almost a hundred leagues, all was under the regal sway of these towers, these peaks, these teeth, these horns, all these needles, all these spires with their snows and their glaciers. Some of them were slender and came to a sharp point, some were rounded, others square, still others like walls; some leaned, some stood erect; some were perched high up on ridges; some were isolated and leapt up from the plain in a single bound; some were white, some pink and some silvery.

And over there is Monte Leone in Italy, while at the opposite horizon, there are peaks lost in the mist whose names he didn't know, somewhere in Dauphiné. How many does that make? How many does that make altogether? For he tried to count them, then he got lost in the numbers. Then he tried to name them in order. "That's Mont Rose, those are the Mischabels, and that's the Lyskamm, right? Next comes the Breithorn, then the Weisshorn, then there's the Cervin, then the Dent d'Hérens, the Dent Blanche and the Grand Cornier..." He changed languages three times. He started with Italian, went on to German, and finished up with French. "But what about you? Do you change? Because I know you well, you're called the Colon... Now *you* I'm more familiar with, because we're getting close to home, with the Pigne d'Arolla, the Ruinette, the Combins, the Vélan, then the Jorasses, Mont Dolent; here too is that nest, that pocket full of crystals—all the Aiguilles: the Verte, the Rouge, the Argentière, the Dru, the Tour, and now I'm here in my own home."

It was right in front of him, or nearly so. "Hah! I know you well," he said, "but you, do you recognize me? ..."

Due south, a great valley opened wide, then, a little farther off, split in half and continued as two branches. When he was just a little boy, he was already going out in the middle of the night with his father, who had a disassembled carbine in his sack while he, the boy, carried their provisions in another sack. "Hah! Here you are. I see you, I see you clearly, but do you recognize me? ... Well," he said, "try to guess who I am. I've stayed the same, you see. I've remained faithful to you. The fact is, if you haven't changed, neither have I... You don't worry about what's forbidden and what's permitted, which means that everything is permitted. You have your chamois and you say, 'Come and shoot them, if you can...' You have gold and you say, 'Come and take it from me...'"

He went on with his speech, saying, "It's a fair fight and, at least with you, a person's above the laws and the regulations..."

They glittered in the light, the mountains, changing color and lighting as the sun rose. He saw the shadows moving slowly, and one of them, which had been lying down, was sitting up, then it was standing up and stretching like a man who had slept. He watched as another one climbed swiftly up a steep incline; when it arrived at the summit, it vanished into the air. There is one mountain that is like a woman removing her gray caraco. Another one is holding a mirror in front of her; the mirror moves in her hand. There are those that are stretched out completely naked, displaying their vast bodies and beautiful coloring, or merely their bosoms with their nipples a shade deeper pink. For the more Farinet gazed at them, the more they came to life, little by little. Some of them turned towards him now, and certain ones gestured to him, whereupon he spoke again. "Well, then, what do you think? What do I have to do? For my part, I know very well what I have to do, but maybe you have a different opinion..."

Watching the entire congregation of mountains as they shifted and rose up in the light, he was moved to speak to them. He said, "The thing is, I've already been in prison in Italy, then they put me in the *galleys* in Sion. And I got out of their prison all by myself, and they couldn't hold onto me very long in their *galleys*, either, because of what you've taught me — yes, you," he said, "you towers, you horns, you needles, pillars of freedom!"

Clouds rose beyond the mountain range, there where the road runs towards Aosta and Italy, and where the monks of the Great Saint Bernard Pass are with their dogs, the ones that have kegs on their necks.

He said, "What do I have to do?"

He posed his question to the mountains. He was turned towards the great Aiguilles and he saw black clouds rising, as often happens in summertime, yet they (the mountains) remained fully illuminated and pure as he posed his question.

They are people, truly they are, these mountains, and they know better than we do what we need. And look how great and powerful they are. Then, leaning towards the chalet, he said, "See what a man is next to them. You can barely see one at the distance those men are from me. He's just a speck, he's tiny, he plays it safe, he's cautious and afraid…"

There was one mountain, with a head and shoulders, taller than the rest and visible from the waist up. The shadow of a cloud passed over it.

Then all of a sudden the shadow retreated, and he saw the mountain rock back and forth: it nodded its head as if to say yes.

VI

Now, a few days afterward, one evening when he was returning to the chalet a little later than usual, he saw the master, who was seated on a bench next to the door, stand up when he caught sight of him.

The master came to meet him.

"Ah! Just the person I was waiting for. You missed a visitor."

"Ah!" said Farinet and stopped short.

He went on, "Can I stay, or should I go back? ...The gendarmes..."

"Oh," said the master, "you can stay. The gendarmes, we haven't seen a single one since the other day."

The two men came together. The master now seemed a little embarrassed. Farinet said to him, "Well, then, who is it?"

"Guess."

"How am I supposed to guess? Is it Ardèvaz?"

"No," said the master. "You're on the wrong track. Looking in the wrong drawer..."

Then he said, "It wasn't a man."

They were walking side by side. It would soon be dark.

"Ah, that's right," said Farinet.

He too was a little embarrassed.

"Did she give you her name?"

"Yes."

"Did you know who she was?"

"Vaguely. I recalled having seen her at Crittin's."

"Oh, she's a good girl, and she's quite devoted to me. So," he said...

"Well, then, you know she's not happy. She says that by now you should have come down several days ago, because everything is ready."

"Oh, yes," he said then, a bit dejectedly, "I'll have to go down."

"And," said the master, "she wanted desperately to go and find you up there, because she had some things to give you, but I told her, 'That's not possible, Mademoiselle, it's no place for a woman up there.' So she waited for you. Yes, until six o'clock... And then she left again, because she couldn't wait any longer, but she left her basket... Just now..."

At this point, the master stopped short, because they were about to arrive at the chalet. Lowering his voice, he said, "She says to tell you that she'll hang a bed sheet in the window under the roof. And if the sheet is there, it means you can come..."

Farinet nodded his head. They went inside the chalet. Farinet sat down in front of the fire.

The master brought him the basket.

"Thanks," said Farinet.

The master watched him on the sly. Farinet lifted the white cloth covering the contents.

All of a sudden, Farinet said, "Well, I'll be able to do something with this."

He pulled two bottles out of the basket and put them next to him where they stood, half-yellow and half-black, half in the light and half in shadow. But there were still other things hidden from view in the basket. He took them out as well. They included a fresh round loaf of bread — a real treat for a man living off his stash of dry bread for six weeks and more.

Right away, he took out his knife and cut into the loaf. First he offered a slice to each of the children, even though they had had supper, then a slice to each of the men there, even though they too had already eaten. There was also some ham in the basket, and everyone got a slice, including the master. They tried to refuse, but saw that Farinet insisted. He served himself last, when they were all seated around the fireplace on two benches joined end to end. They began eating almost without saying a word, while it grew totally dark outside. Then Farinet also uncorked the bottles. He filled a glass and held it out to the master, who said, "To your health!" and emptied it in three gulps.

Then the glass was passed around according to custom, from the eldest to the youngest, with Farinet drinking last.

All of a sudden, he spoke up again.

"Well, yes, I'm going to go down tomorrow or the day after."

There was nothing left of the bread or the ham. He sent the glass around one last time.

"The thing is, I've got a nice setup down there... It'll be a long time before they find me. I have three ways out... Besides, right now I have more dust than I need." He pointed at his waist, where two fat lumps showed beneath his pants.

"I really have to get down to work..."

They said, "To your health!"

He said, "To your health!"

It was pitch dark; the fire, like another sun, was beginning to sink, because no one was tending it anymore.

Farinet turned to Félicien and said, "You'll get one — one of my coins."

"Oh, thank you very much," said Félicien.

Farinet seemed a little downcast, and they could barely see him. Then he turned to Félicien's brother, whose name was Pierre.

"You, too."

"Oh, thank you very much," said Pierre.

VII

Joséphine shut the door behind her at the rear of the house. Unfortunately, it creaked a bit, being old and poorly oiled, but at this hour everyone in the village was already asleep.

For the past two days now the bed sheet had been hanging in the window.

She crossed the yard down to the old fortress wall. Its line could be followed readily with the eye and was legible all the way to the tower, even on a dark night.

For two days now, she had been waiting for him.

The moon was not up, but there were many stars out; above her, they studded the colorless sky with gleaming points — white, a little yellow, even green or red. She saw behind her the façades of the houses, leaning against one another; they were full of holes, which were the windows, and these holes were dark — except for one, and just then its light went out.

She listened, but there was not a sound, all manner of wind having quieted down and the lives of man and animal having all gone quiet (the chickens in their coops, the dogs attached to their chains or shut up in the kitchen for the night). A profound silence. And then, within it, when she listened more carefully, there rose — as if born from this very silence — a muffled roar, coming from who knew where, a kind of long-drawn-out sighing breath with no beginning or end: the Rhône, out there in the plain. That was all.

She set forth again.

She went along, into the sound and the darkness mingled together; she went along, into this vast silence. She went along, into air that was rather cool and smelled dry, then humid in the places that had just been watered. It was fragrant, fragrant with every kind of scent — of flowers or plants, thyme, marjoram, laurel. And this sang to her inside her head. And this danced for her inside her head. In the middle of the vast night, she is going along and she is all alone, and for two evenings now she has been waiting for him, but perhaps this evening he will be back.

At one point, she saw emerge before her, as it disentangled itself from the unbroken darkness, the tower lopsided like a candle that has burned down askew. She stands still.

She can hear her heart knocking against her ribs, like some-one asking to go out. Perhaps he really will have come down. For she had already come the night before and the night before that, all in vain, but perhaps today... Knock, knock, and then the Rhône. She started walking again, among all sorts of rocks scattered about and interspersed with bushes that she had to go around. But all the while, up above, the tower beckoned to her, calling to her, saying, "This way...to the right, and now to the left." Thus, she was led to the foot of the tower. And right away she saw that he had returned, because the sack she had hidden the night before, beneath the barberry bush at the entrance to the underground passage, was no longer there. The sack is no longer there! He's here. The fact is shouted silently in her head, then her heart resumes making noise. She came to a stop again and leaned for a moment against the rock wall to pull herself together. Then she bent down and ducked the upper half of her body into an opening there. "Oh my God!" she thinks suddenly. "I've forgotten the handkerchiefs!" She had, the night before, brought him some clothes, and the handkerchiefs were missing. She had promised herself to bring them this evening. She sees that she doesn't have them, which brings her up short again, filled with sad-ness—ah! how mixed up we are inside!—then brimming with happiness, because he is here. That's what matters, that's the only thing that matters, after so many months of being apart...

He is free, he is here. That's all she needs as she sets forth again, into this passage where she could just squeeze her way through. There was something hard right up against her left shoulder, and against the right one as well, and likewise above her, skimming her back. She reached out with her right hand and felt the rock face in front of her; with her foot, she tested the floor beneath her, because it was becoming ever steeper and more uneven.

She said to herself, "It'll be ten months." She repeated the phrase: Ten months! … Then, as she advanced, all of these things got more and more muddled together in her head. Finally, she was brought to a second opening between her feet.

"Tô!"

This is a mountain call. It is what the shepherds shout to one another, from one end of the pasture to the other, or even from one pasture to another above the valley, in the free air, beneath the wide-open sky. Now it is shouted downwards into the darkness, yet her heart is leaping, because he is going to come and he is going to answer, because he is here.

And "Tô!" one more time.

Then, from far away and coming by the same path — muffled, yet at the same time protected and preserved by the narrowness of the shaft — a voice came: "Tô!"

A voice — and then it is him now, because she can hear a stone creaking.

Due to the echo, the noise sounds very close and very far away at the same time, clear and feeble at first, then louder but muffled; then it becomes a mere murmur again. "Tô!" she says, and there comes the reply: "Tô!"

Then, five or six meters below her, a big rock that jutted out turned faintly red.

"Listen," she said at this moment, "I'd come down, but I can't find the ladder."

And the voice that replied to her was distant and close at the same time.

"I took it away. Hold on, I'm coming…"

He was indeed coming; he kept on coming, for the light reappeared, more vividly, on the same rock and then on the rocks surrounding it, and passed from one to the next while growing brighter. And the voice said, "Are you still there?" And she replied, "Yes." Then, abruptly, the light has risen up the shaft to her level, and a hand appears.

This hand held a storm lantern.

She has no need to lean forward much in order to see that he is coming up now, that it is him. For it is his fate to be, at times, in the airy heights above men, at times beneath them in the depths of the earth.

"Oh, Farinet, you've come back! …"

He said simply, "As you can see."

"When?"

"Just now."

"Oh!" she said. "Oh, Farinet, you've come back…"

But he—his torso having now reached the level of her feet—he hasn't even raised his head, as he was clenching the lantern between his teeth the whole time. As a result, she sees him, she can see him perfectly well, while he can't see her and seems not to mind it; but perhaps that's because he's too busy hooking the top of the ladder onto an oaken peg. Then he spoke again, between his teeth.

"All set. You can come."

He climbs back down the ladder.

Gingerly, she extends one leg, then the other, into the void.

"Oh! You know what?" she said as she descended the ladder. "I forgot your handkerchiefs!"

He said nothing in reply. She said, "Did you find your clothes in the sack?"

"Yes."

And rung by rung she descended, then he was there and she was there — reunited again, and after such a long time joined together, so tightly that they were pressed up against each other; but as he put the lamp down at his feet, the only thing he said was, "Watch out, I'm going to drop the ladder... Move off a little to one side."

She kept her feelings to herself; she followed him submissively. He led the way. He was no more than a black shape, nearly filling the entire diameter of the passageway with his body, which was fringed by just enough empty space to allow the lantern's wan light to filter through. An uncomfortable place, an ominous place, she said to herself, yet she marveled all the while. It is hewn from the rock, just enough to allow one person to pass through, but not two. Over time, the rock beds must have slipped in places, for he would say, "Watch your head!" or "Be careful where your put your foot!" At still other times, he would extend his arm behind him, bringing the lantern towards her, which didn't prevent her from bumping into things at every turn. This lasted a long time, as they went down and down.

Then, all of a sudden, she saw Farinet stand up straight. She too stands up.

All at once the air had become fresher, while a shaft of light — no longer just that from Farinet's lantern — illuminated the rock wall some distance ahead of them. It formed a kind of pocket, the other end of which faced the open air above the gorge.

It was spacious and seemed wholesome. Clearly, Farinet was going to be well accommodated, even exceptionally so. He was obviously well supplied, for he lacked for nothing. A bucket had been placed beneath a little spring that could be heard dripping in one corner. There was a fireplace with a stovepipe, and next to it a stack of dry wood. In another corner on a slab, there was a new straw mattress with woolen blankets. Finally, on a second slab, smooth and flat as a table, with a square-hewn rock serving as a chair in front of it, all the materials needed for the job were laid out: a blowtorch, plaster molds, a chunk of charcoal, bottles of acid and some tools.

Without so much as a pause, he went straight to his workbench, where he turns around.

"Did you remember the spirits of wine?"[4]

That was all.

At that, she began to feel a tiny ache in a place beneath her caraco, on the left side, beneath the caraco, then beneath her blouse and perhaps even a little deeper still. She hadn't said a word. She waited. Ah! Now there was room, all the room in the world, much more than was needed, but he had turned his back to her and sat down. And now, already separated from him by space, she was separated as well by a faint noise, like a slight rustling of silk; it was the water flowing, deep and smooth, fifty meters below at the bottom of the gorge. Hence it was necessary to raise one's voice a little, and he raised his voice a little to speak to her. Separated from him by space, separated from him by the noise, separated still more by something else (she didn't quite know what it was), she was there the while and she gazed at him.

He had picked up one of his leather pouches. He emptied it carefully into a small iron box.

"The thing is, I have to get back to work right away. I don't have a single coin left... Did Crittin tell you how much I owed him?"

"Oh, there's no rush."

"Sure there is," he said. "Ah, I found the spirits of wine."

The bottle was in front of him.

She saw him in profile. Farinet was blowing on the flame. Whatever was left of the shadows between the vaulted ceiling and the storm lantern swiftly fled from all directions into the nooks and crannies. A bright beam of light delineated his face in the greatest detail: his moustache, which had turned russet, his puffed-out cheek and a vein that swelled likewise on the side of his neck. The brim of his hat cast a deep shadow over him. Then his cheeks fell back and the light immediately fell, while the flame of the blow-torch stood up, soft and buoyant. By the lantern's motionless light, fainter still and paler than before, Joséphine saw indistinctly that he was pouring something into a mold.

Abruptly, he spoke again.

"Did they come today?"

"No."

"What about yesterday?"

"No."

"I guess they've had enough already." (He was speaking of the gendarmes.) "Well, then, tell Crittin, I'll come by one of these evenings soon…"

But he left off, because he had begun to blow again, while the light increased once more, projecting his figure onto the vault overhead. It was misshapen, huge and without neck or head, despite being clearly outlined.

Then everything went dark again.

She was barely visible now, being of the same shade of gray as the rock and the shadows, from which she emerged only to re-enter them almost immediately. It seemed as though she moved forward only to go back again. She stood immobile, her hands crossed in front of her apron — still immobile for a long moment against the rock wall. But the spasm of pain passed beneath her ribs again, as when one has rheumatism, the way it happens to old people when bad weather is coming. In the midst of her disordered thoughts, she said to herself, "What's the matter with him?" She said to herself, "Is there something wrong? He hasn't kissed me, he hasn't even said hello to me."

"Oh!" At that, she stiffens up a little.

"Oh!" she went on. "Maybe he's had enough of me. Maybe it's all ancient history already" (as she continued to stir up old ideas and memories). "Maybe — and I wasn't able to see it — but already in Sion, before they put him in the *galleys*…"

"Oh! Farinet…"

She said this out loud and is surprised to hear her own voice, as if she were not the one who had uttered this cry.

He turns around, puzzled, but she shook her head and he didn't recognize her (in the dim lantern light), because she had changed, because she had become taller.

"What's the matter with you?" he said. "Are you getting impatient?" The thing is, you see, I need some coins and I don't know what's wrong this evening… It's not working."

"I can see, Farinet, that you clearly don't care for me anymore."

She kept shaking her head. She took a step forward, then abruptly turned away. She lifted her hands and hid her face, which grew narrow between them.

He stood up, casting a shadow that reached her, across the bright sand, the soft sand.

"Come on, Joséphine! "Come on, now!"

"No. All you think about is your gold, not me."

"But," he said. "Come on…"

And he didn't know what else to say. And she went on, "No, no, just about your gold, Farinet, and about yourself." Her head in her hands, she turns away from him.

"Ten months," she said, "ten months... No, no, leave me alone, leave me alone, Farinet..."

But this time he came up to her and took her by the shoulder. He said, "You're out of your mind!"

He said, "Come on now, come on now!" Because, after all, he had a good heart, he drew her to him and took her by the hand.

He said, "Come on now, show me your face... Come on now! ..."

But all of a sudden it was he who was seized bodily, for she had flung herself against him. "Oh!" she said. "Is it true? Is it really true?"

Farinet's pipe fell to the ground. She held his face tight against her own, she warmed him with her warmth.

"Oh," she said, "I love to wait on you..."

She held out her mouth; she said, "Oh, is it true? Oh, is it really true? ...Oh, forgive me, Farinet... I thought" — meanwhile he was moving backwards.

They were next to the straw mattress; he nearly fell over. She said, "It's just that I love you. It's just that I love you." But the words on her lips became slurred, then they ceased altogether...

How much time had passed, he couldn't have said. For a moment he didn't even know where he was. He hadn't opened his eyes yet and in his head, befogged with dreams, there was no room for reality. He wondered, "Where am I?" At first he answered himself sadly, "In the *galleys*." But at that moment a puff of fresh air passed over his face. "No, in the chalet." He felt happiness in his heart. Then everything changes once more, due to a smell of kerosene that he had just become conscious of — the storm lantern had gone out for lack of fuel. And the sadness returned when he said to himself, "I'm in the cave"; at the same moment, he felt something warm next to him. This time he opened his eyes, but he didn't move. Since the straw bed was set back a little, he had to get accustomed to the half-darkness, in whose depths he lay on his back and gazed uncomprehendingly up at the vault overhead, which the darkness and the feeble light divided between them. Then all at once he lowered his eyes; then she was there, then he recognized her. "Ah, yes," he said to himself, "it's her, ah, yes, she came with the supplies…" He was sad all over again.

He edged away from her slightly, because of the warmth of this body that was too close to his. He could see her indistinctly; he was able to see that she was asleep.

He could see her better and better — her large, smooth face, the skin of her forehead pulled back by her hair, which was braided so tightly that it hadn't come undone, and her puckered lips. It was plain to see that she was happy. She was happy now. Happy, confident, quite abandoned to sleep, filled with contentment. Her deep, calm respiration raised her chest beneath the brown-wool blanket in a regular rhythm, like that of a ticking clock. Once, twice; one stroke, another one; and from the midst of the sound of the water, there also came the sound of her breathing, which he could hear, so close was he to her.

Suddenly he became annoyed at this.

He said to himself, "She's still here. What time is it?"

When he went to get his watch from his vest pocket, he saw that he had taken the vest off. Turning around, he spotted it, tossed on the ground next to the bed. Then he made a sweeping gesture to get hold of it, and she came uncovered, exposing her bare shoulder. He said to himself, "So much the better. That'll wake her up." A stout shoulder, round and full, and the arm below it was of two colors, brown and white. One could see her neck, which was brown and white. One could see that she had a brown face and a white throat. But he was searching impatiently for his watch; rummaging in all of his vest pockets at random until he found the right one, he sees that it is three o'clock. "Joséphine! Hey, Joséphine! ..." She didn't hear him. She was still smiling. He took her by the shoulder and shook her. "Hey! Joséphine, it's time!"

Her breathing was interrupted, while her smooth eyelids slowly retracted to reveal the globes of her eyes, vacant at first.

But soon they were filled anew with consciousness, and the smile that had never left her mouth ascended to them, and her eyes smiled.

She held her arms out to him. But he, sitting on the edge of the straw bed next to her, he said, "None of that. Joséphine, none of that! It's time, you know. It'll be light soon."

"None of that!" he went on. "None of that! You need to get dressed. Do you want to get me caught?"

VIII

Meanwhile, the life of the country went on as always and nothing happened during the month that followed.

They lead modest lives here; they don't live large. A man was making his way up to his vineyard.

In a garden, a woman can be seen tugging on Swiss chard leaves, big, curly leaves — almost black, due to their green color and the broad white band in the middle along the midrib.

One could see old man Bruchet going to sit under the sundial whose needle had fallen off and whose numerals were faded. The sundial itself was not visible, at least not in the glare of the sun. From time to time, the mule from the chalet would arrive with Félicien; it was a young animal with a red coat, quite rotund beneath its pack, which made it rounder still and rendered its legs slim. It would bring butter and cheese and go back up with a supply of bread, matches, soap and semolina for making soup.

And from time to time, one could also see the gendarmes, because they were still chasing around the countryside. Usually in pairs, they went at a walking pace, their capes rolled up around their torsos and their pistols slung from their belts; they were dressed in their black uniforms with red epaulettes. They would make the rounds of the village and go up to Farinet's house. And sometimes one or the other would say, "Do you seriously think we don't know where he's hiding?…"

Sometimes, when they encountered a man from the village on the road, they would ask him, "You still haven't seen him?"

And he would say, "Nope."

But they would shrug their shoulders.

"Don't get the idea we're that stupid. We know well enough he's not far away. Only he might pull off some nasty stunt. That could cost us more trouble than it's worth. So for now we're just going to keep an eye on him..."

There were indeed some in the village who also knew where Farinet's hideout was, but none of them had ever been there. They talked about it from hearsay. It was understood that Farinet had his house (where he hadn't lived for a long time now, where he would probably live less and less, with an untended garden, a vine arbor never pruned, and a few fruit trees that had gone back to nature) — he had his house, where he might or might not be; his other arrangements were his own business.

"It's a lucky thing they built the citadel way back when," said Fontana, "because he's gotten to take advantage of it. It used to come in handy during a siege, but now it's been even more useful to him, for making his coins. His house — everyone knows about it; it wouldn't have been wise...While down there (here he lowered his voice), he can be undisturbed, so long as he stays put and keeps his head down... Because he can count on us..."

They nodded their heads.

"He has three ways out: by way of the house, under the tower and by the gorge. And the gorge has its own ways out, too. Why, there are as many as a man could want. The gorge, that's means the whole countryside, especially at night, and for a fellow who knows it the way he does, a fellow who's quick on his feet, young, strong and clever..."

It was towards ten o'clock in the evening in Crittin's café when Farinet came for the first time to join the three or four men, always the same ones, who were there. They were overjoyed to see him again in good health, openly thumbing his nose at the government and the gendarmes.

Once again, he was going out at night, with freedom as his companion. And, with her[5] as his companion, he entered the café that evening. As he opened the door, he also let in a good gust of fresh air.

"Good evening," he said. "How are things? … They aren't here, are they? That's good! … Crittin," he said, "I've brought you some coins…"

They went to sit down in the kitchen behind the closed shutters. There he began telling the story of his escape: the file, the bars, the descent of the wall, the moon, the paths, and how the roosters, who were already crowing, spread the tale of his victory from village to village.

He drank with us and left towards midnight. He and Crittin agreed on a signal (like Joséphine's bed sheet) that would show him that he could come without fear: a watering can that Crittin would turn upside down on a pole at the bottom of the garden.

As for supplies, that was Joséphine's affair.

So everything seemed to be arranged, even very well arranged. Why, then, were they taken aback, a few days later, by the way he looked? He seemed sad and discouraged.

This was at the beginning of August, one evening when all five of them were there at Crittin's.

"Has anyone ever had a reason to complain about me?" he began. "Have I ever done anything wrong to anyone?"

 "What about you, Charrat?" he asked.

Charrat shook his head.

"Or maybe you, Ardèvaz?"

Ardèvaz shrugged.

"Well, could it be you, Fontana?"

Old man Fontana held up his hand.

"Me!"

And letting it fall, he slapped the table.

"As for me, you've never done me anything but good turns…"

That left Crittin. Farinet said to him, "You're last."

Crittin said nothing in reply, but went over to an old pot sitting in a corner of the fireplace and raised the lid. Inside it, there was a piece of cloth folded into quarters.

"I have faith in you… Well, you can see where I keep it!"

This was in the kitchen of the inn, after the place had closed. The doors of the house had been locked shut and all the lights extinguished except for the lamp that illuminated the men, but it couldn't be seen from outside, because of the shutters made of solid wood. If anyone came and made it necessary to open the door, Farinet would have time to escape by way of the attic and the roof, for they had fore-seen everything and even left the door to the stairs open. It was an ancient kitchen, low-ceilinged, with a slate floor. In the middle there was a large table, around which they were seated. There were two benches, with three men on one of them and two on the other, on opposite sides of the table. Joséphine, for her part, was seated in a dark corner, beneath the projecting hood of the fireplace.

"Well, then, if that's the case," Farinet went on, "if you have no complaints about me, if no one here has a complaint about me, what more does the government want? Here it is, going on four years now they can't think of anything better to do than cause me trouble. And it's gone on for too long and caused me too much trouble!"

He was talking; he talked a lot. He must have had few occasions to do so, all day long in his cave — so they said to themselves. They let him talk.

"Is my gold counterfeit or not? It's been examined by the experts, not once, but three, four times. It's gold, as true as true can be, pure gold, virgin gold — it's gold that's worth a lot more than the government's… *I'll* tell you what it is: the government's jealous. Its laws, they're made for its benefit… We could make a nice little life for ourselves around here, couldn't we, with our own money and not theirs?…"

It was apparent, that evening, that Farinet was seeking to justify himself and also to find a way out of a situation that offered scant prospect of having one.

"Maybe you're going to tell me that I'm not from the commune, but, really now, how many years have I been here? It's going on seven, eight years… Eight years that I haven't left, or at least not voluntarily. (He laughed.) So I am from here, a little bit anyway. Besides, I have a house here, don't I? Granted, it's not worth much anymore. (He laughed.) Well, we should try to get organized, to organize something…"

"Yes," said Fontana, "that's my opinion."

"Ah, it's a shame," said Farinet, "that I went to Aosta. That's what spoiled everything. If I hadn't gotten myself arrested by the king of Italy, they never would have dared to arrest me here."

"Never," said Crittin, "because nobody would have wanted to turn you in."

"And in Sion, too, I wasn't too smart… It's my fault, I know it. You weren't in Sion. I was all alone…"

At this moment, they heard a movement in the corner of the room, and a voice said, "What about me?"

It was Joséphine.

Until then she had kept apart and done nothing to draw attention to herself — quite the contrary. With her arms on her knees and her head set forward, she had kept still in her corner, halfway beneath the hood of the chimney. Surprised, they all looked in her direction.

He, too, was surprised. He said, "Of course, you were there."

"And after that, Farinet, didn't I help you?"

"That's true," said Farinet.

"Would you have gotten out of the *galleys* without me?"

Again he had to say, "That's true," at which she fell silent.

He wanted to go on, but he had a hard time finding the right words now. It was Fontana who spoke up.

"There's just one thing, Farinet. If I were you, I'd keep an eye on my escape routes."

"Oh," said Farinet, "there are mines everywhere."

Ardévaz put in, "Me, I wouldn't stick around here too long. They've got to know where you're hiding. In your shoes, I'd go back up to the chalet."

"Oh, I'll go back up all right, but I had to make my coins. The first few days, I don't know what was wrong, it wasn't going right, but now it's going just fine."

He said, "it's going just fine," but his looks said he didn't believe it. He went on, "Besides, from here it's easy to see them coming."

He started to laugh. All at once, he was in a cheerful mood again. He turned to Joséphine.

"Isn't that so, Joséphine? What can you see from your window?"

"Me?"

"Yes, when you're up there in your room, looking towards the valley."

Now she was the one who seemed surprised.

"I don't know."

And the others were all surprised, but he said, "Try again."

"I see the water, the land, the sky…"

"What do you see out your window, Joséphine, when you're up there, under the roof?"

"I see the mountains, I see the Rhône…"

"And along the Rhône?"

"There's Saxon."

"And between Saxon and here?"

"There's the road."

"And on the road?"

Then the penny dropped, and they all started to laugh,[6] while she said, "On the road there are some dots."

"What color?"

"Black."

"Shiny?"

"Shiny."

"Well, then, they can be seen from a distance, right? That's good. Let's talk about something else."

He drew his coin pouch from his pocket.

"Do you want to see my coins, the ones I had to remake? They were too white at first, and not smooth enough. But now, it seems to me… What do you think of them?"

IX

Be that as it may, a week or so later (and it had been a good three or four days since anyone had seen a single gendarme in the vicinity of the village), Romailler sent word to Farinet that he would be pleased to have him pay a visit, because he needed to talk to him.

It was not Joséphine to whom he had entrusted the message, but rather Crittin, who took Farinet aside and passed it on to him.

" Romailler would like to talk to you... Romailler, the councillor...You worked for him back in the day."

"What does he want with me?"

"I don't know, but he's expecting you one of these evenings."

Farinet shook his head.

"If I were you, I'd go," said Crittin. "You never know. Romailler has a long reach. And he guarantees you can come without fear, because he's taken precautions of his own."

But Farinet shook his head again. All the same, the next day, as he was waiting for Joséphine, he suddenly recalled Romailler's proposal. He was underground. This couldn't go on much longer, he thought. He told himself that he risked nothing in going to see Romailler (whom he trusted), this evening beneath the beautiful sky and the first stars. True, Joséphine was supposed to be coming, but I'll explain it to her... Perhaps the very idea that he would thus have an excuse for not being there was an added temptation, as he took up his rifle (for he rarely parted with it). He rolled up the rope ladder and hid it together with the storm lantern in one of the recesses of the passage. He made his way cautiously beneath the sky, among the scattered boulders and the bramble bushes. Before venturing out into the open, he made doubly sure that no one was around to spy on him. From the top of the vineyards, beneath the light of the stars, the view swept the exposed ground and thoroughly reassured him. He had no need of a path to find his way. He could see the white house from a distance. Romailler's house stood a little to the east and a little above the village; it was new, with a whitewashed, stone foundation. The shutters were closed; no light was visible in the windows. Nonetheless, Farinet went up the stone staircase and was about to knock on the door when it opened partway and Romailler stepped forward. He sees Farinet and says, "Ah, it's you! Come in, I've been expecting you." He held out his hand.

They crossed the kitchen, then entered a room off to one side where there was a table and some chairs.

"Have a seat," said Romailler.

Farinet sat down without saying a word. Romailler began by offering him a cigar, which Farinet took, while Romailler struck a match. Then Romailler said, "So, how are you?"

"Fine, thank you."

"It's been a while since we last saw each other. Do you remember when you used to work for me? How long has it been (he counted up)? A lot's happened since then."

He lit himself a cigar and took a drag on it.

"And that's just it, my boy. You must realize that your situation won't be tenable much longer. All it would take would be for them to know where you're hiding, and perhaps they already do. And suppose you did manage to get away, where would you want to go, my boy? The chalets up high, they're fine for the summer, but we're already in August; soon it'll be fall. You can't get out of the country, because they're on the lookout for you everywhere. You'll have to hunker down in your hideaway… So hear me out. I have a proposition to make to you…"

He flicked the ash from his cigar.

"The point is, there are the liberals," Romailler went on...
"Perhaps you haven't read their newspaper, because hardly
anybody reads it around here. You see, they're the opposition. Well, they're saying that the government could arrest
you if it wanted to, but it's not doing so on purpose. That's
because we're conservative around here, same as it is. And
because we're all your friends... The liberals say the government is afraid that if it arrested you, it'd lose our votes in
the elections... You follow me?"

Farinet nodded.

"And that's awkward...it's awkward for the government. I'm
convinced that if the government wanted to, it could arrest
you tomorrow, but that would cost some money and maybe
a few lives. Well, then, listen closely... I've been instructed
to tell you that you should turn yourself in. The government would take that into account. You've already done
six months in the *galleys*, which would be deducted... God
knows, you wouldn't have more than, say, six months to do,
and six months pass quickly in the wintertime... Then you
could go home and live in peace; you wouldn't owe a thing
to anyone ... But it would be on one condition..."

Romailler paused again.

"And this condition would be that you give up making and
circulating your coins. That's the main condition ..."

Farinet burst out, "Well, the answer's no!"

But Romailler wouldn't allow himself to be interrupted.

"I know very well that you think your gold is good. But
there are laws. Do you realize what would happen if everyone started acting like you? How would we manage things?
... There are laws, and a legal code. All they would ask of
you is to respect it in the future..."

Farinet said, "Well, the answer's still no!"

"Hold on," said Romailler, "not so fast..."

At that, he called out, shouting, "Hey, there, Thérèse!"

There came the noise of a chair being moved by someone in the room overhead, followed by the sound of footsteps. Then the door opened.

Farinet did not immediately see her, because he had his back turned to her.

Romailler said, "Come here, Thérèse." When she had come and stood by his side, he said, "This is my daughter. Don't you recognize her?"

Farinet made no reply.

"Ah, that's because she's at that age where young women change fast," said Romailler with a laugh. "She's a young lady. That's what you are, Thérèse, a young lady."

She flushed quite pink above her silk blouse, which was blue like the sky. Farinet still said nothing, so Romailler said to his daughter, "Listen, Thérèse, go and get us a bottle of *fendant*."

She said, "Yes, father." She leaves the room; she goes away. Romailler said nothing more. She came back with the bottle, but now Farinet didn't dare to look at her again.

She put the bottle and the glasses on the table. He didn't dare to look at her, but he continued to see her in his heart.

He heard Romailler's voice.

"Thank you very much, Thérèse... I think we have everything we need, you can go..."

Farinet hears her leave; he hears her footsteps recede; then there was a moment of silence while Romailler uncorked the bottle, which he held clamped between his knees.

He filled the two glasses.

"It's good, isn't it? And perhaps you recognize it, Farinet. You helped make it...back in the day."

Taking a swig of wine between his lips, he swished it around two or three times under his palate without swallowing (so as to extract all of the taste).

"Ah, it's not half bad. What do you think of it?" he repeated, because Farinet had made no reply. "But good wine, you see — you have to be able to drink it in peace..."

Farinet wanted to say something in reply.

"No, don't say anything. You have three weeks to make up your mind. You have from now until the end of the month. Think it over! Because today... Today, you say no because you have your pride; tomorrow you'd want to say yes, and tomorrow you'd no longer be able to... You have three weeks. And during this time you have nothing to fear... Of course, you'd be better off if you didn't show yourself in the village square in broad daylight, in case the gendarmes were in the neighborhood, and you didn't go out of your way to taunt them. But apart from this one condition, they'll leave you alone, I give you my word... Don't say anything... Your health!"

They clinked glasses once again.

Farinet stood up.

"Another glass?"

"No," he said. "I should go."

"Just one."

He shook his head.

"Well, then, that's settled. You'll bring me your answer by the end of the month."

There was no longer anything but the night and the stars — that is, in front of him, behind him and above him. "No!" Farinet said "no" one more time and, having crossed the hedgerow, he followed it on the other side, in the thick grass, in the damp grass, where there were glowworms like slivers fallen from the moon. He had hidden his rifle in a bush before going into Romailler's house; he went first thing to retrieve it. And it was as if he was once again himself—for a moment he had ceased to be so. He wondered, "Since when?" Since... But he didn't look into it further, as he stood facing the valley. And once again he said to himself, "Turn myself in, me! Perhaps they thought I was for sale! A glass of wine and a cigar, that's a bargain." He gave a little laugh, with his hands in his pockets. He walked slowly now, because he could see that, about these decisions he faced, it wasn't all that simple... After descending the length of the hedgerow, he reached the vineyards. He was immersed in an ashen moonlight, a light, gray eiderdown of moonlight that spoke of the sweetness of life. He saw that it could be sweet; he saw this for the first time. This made him feel tired, while at the same time he was happy.

Why happy? "Aha," he said to himself, "it's because it would be so easy if I said yes. You come out, you mix with other men, you no longer have anything to fear from them."

Towards eleven o'clock at night, in the middle of the meadows, beneath the moon, he wondered, "What's happened?"

He sat down, the better to ponder this. Turning around, he looked to see whether there was still a light up there, but Romailler's house was already hidden behind a rise. He said to himself, "Perhaps." He looked below him, in the grayness of the moonlight, at the rooftops jammed together as one; down below, the people were together and slept peacefully. Meanwhile, he was under the earth or high up in the air—is that what freedom is? For him there was no middle ground, yet now freedom might be in the middle; that too was what he was telling himself. He was seated beneath the gray moon with peaks of white mountains on all sides. And I am condemned to be all the way up there (as he sees, when he raises his head) or (he lowers his head) way down there, beneath the ruins of the tower he can see. Under the earth like a mole, up in the air like an eagle. A man (he said to himself then), isn't he meant to be lying under a roof, between the stars and the earth, in a bed? A man is meant to live with other men, isn't he? And to have a little property, an animal or two, a vineyard. Isn't that so? And a woman.

At that, he started to laugh. "I have one." But then he said to himself, "No, I don't..." A woman of your own choosing, who you liked, who loved you, all white and gentle, in a bedroom, a real bedroom, with a table and a lamp...

Then all of a sudden he got to his feet. "Too bad. Me, I have freedom. That leads us back underground."

He set off again, now going straight down in the direction of the tower. There may be some things that are nice to have, but they're not for me. He shook his head. Yet there was still this big, gray moon where, below him, the houses in Mièges crouched leaning their heads on one another's shoulders to sleep. He sees that he won't be able to go right back into the stale air and the dampness. He also recollects that Joséphine must have waited for him. "She's a good girl," he said to himself, "but..." And here, having reached a point level with his house, he veered to the left. Not far from there, the house is just visible, set back in a kind of thicket — the fruit trees, long since left untended, and all sorts of plants and bushes that have sprung up at their feet. For all that, it is a roof, walls, a room and a bed. I'm not risking anything, and it's Romailler who told me so. I can trust him. No matter how much they searched, there's no way they could have found the key in its hiding place. As he can see, in fact, when he bends down. It's there, all right, underneath one of the front steps. Holding it between his fingers, he can feel how rust has given it a velvety coating over time. He can also see, as he mounts the porch, that the vine that covered the front of the house has become detached, and he gets his feet tangled up in it. Despite this, he goes up the steps, then tries to insert the key in the lock, but he sees that it won't go in anymore. Ah, everything's a fine mess! But so what? It's my home. All these things can be fixed. Then he notices that the door is merely pulled shut, so that all he has to do is lean his shoulder against the panel. As he enters, he lets the dead leaves come in at the same time and gets his face caught in the spider webs hanging between the jambs. That doesn't matter, nor does the darkness into which he plunges, groping his way to the mantelpiece where, he recalls, there is a tin box full of candle ends. He takes one out and strikes a match. He raises the tiny flame over his head; it is blue and still unsteady. First, it dips back down to the tallow to claim its sustenance, then suddenly it gains strength and stands erect, revealing the upset furniture, the two benches turned upside down, the cupboard left wide open, the table itself completely covered with objects tossed there in a disorderly heap — for they had been here. Ah, he can see that very well, but it amuses him, because they won't have discovered a thing anyway. They ransacked the place, looking for his gold and his molds, and they didn't even find the entrance to the underground passage, as he can see when he goes down into the cellar and the barrel blocking the entrance hasn't been moved. They hadn't been clever enough; he finds that amusing. He goes back upstairs. After all, he's in his own home and everything is fine. But what, he said to himself, was he thinking about before? He can't recall.

He set the candle beside him on a chair. Leaning on his elbows, he cast a shadow. It was at this moment that old man Sage appeared. He was seeing old man Sage again in his mind's eye. Weren't those the good old days, when old man Sage slept in this room and he, Farinet, in the one upstairs? Wasn't that already freedom? There is one kind that is gentle and another one that is untamed. Old man Sage is seated in the kitchen before the fire, busy sorting his herbs; there were others hanging in bunches from the beams of the ceiling. Meanwhile, Farinet would be getting his pack ready, taking care to stow his dismantled rifle in the bottom. A rifle that breaks down into two sections comes in handy. On top would go the packets containing all kinds of medicinal plants for those who drink their "herbal elixirs."

He would take the packets as old man Sage handed them to him, until the pack was full. It was a huge pack, tall and wide, yet lightweight, much lighter than one would have thought; it weighed nowhere near as much as he did himself — for there is hardly anything to them, these dried leaves. He would look as though he were under a crushing burden, but he wasn't. He laughs; those were the good old days, weren't they?

He would leave at daybreak; those were the good old days. He wouldn't take the train, in the first place, because it followed a circuitous route, and then because of the rifle, which he would use on the way back (or planned to, at least). Nor would he take the road through the valley. He would set out going straight ahead, not bothering with the trails (when there were any), but going down the slope of the hill, which plunges steeply from the top of the mountain range all the way to the Rhône — from 3,000 meters to 400 meters — through scree, then vineyards, then more vineyards, through orchards, then more orchards. He would set out for Sion, which was entirely gray, then pink on one side and gray on the other, then all golden in front. At first, his shoes would glisten more brightly than those the gendarmes wore in full dress (it was the good Lord who polished them for you, for free, with his dew); then they would turn white, the way they do when you have spent the whole day working in plaster. Everything would be in constant flux during this time, for the land itself also changes continuously, by turns all green, all gray, all bare, or bedecked entirely with flowers and foliage; now quite barren and wild, now like a park filled with girls seated beneath the trees of a Sunday — in the sun, then in the shade, then in the sun. He, too, would be in the sun, then in the shade before a glass of cool wine in the wine cellars, where the local people would invite him to have a drink because he had acquaintances in the villages. Thus he would be conducted from place to place until evening.

Ah, he says to himself, those really were the good old days. He relit a candle end with the one that was about to go out.

And he sees the rest of this story clearly, as if it were this new flame that illuminated it; he sees where it goes wrong (if it truly went wrong, he says to himself). He sees old man Sage getting up one evening, like so, and old man Sage said, "That's not all ...There's more than just the plants. And you, aren't you a little bit like a son to me?"

Old man Sage went to the cupboard in the kitchen. Underneath a pile of old linens, there was an iron box that locked with a key. He held it in his lap. The fire illuminates the whole room, on account of the dry larch branches, still with their needles, that he had just tossed on. He was in full view, the old man, as he went to search in his pants pocket for his coin pouch. And in among the coins there was a tiny key, which he grasped with his aged fingers and put to use.

"Seeing as how you're kind of like my son now, and one never knows what might happen. Well, then, this here is a certificate. As you can see, it's got a signature. That there is another one."

He handed me the papers. I read them. And he said to me, "This will be yours when I'm dead. It's none of the law's business." Next, under the papers, there were some pieces of yellow rock, and under the pieces of rock there was some fine powder that he let trickle through his fingers. "You see?" I saw. "Do you really see?" I see. "You know what this is? This is freedom for men! One of these days, I'll go and show you where to find it, in the rocky places."

He wanted to come and show me himself where it — freedom — is found. It's in the mountains, it's at the very top of them, higher than any plants. We set out before daylight. We ascended by way of the vineyards, then among the rock fields, then through the grass, then among more rocks, and snow. Beautiful blue weather with lots of little white clouds, all going in the same direction as if in a regatta, and above our heads at first, then less and less so, until we arrive inside them. At last, we end up snared in these scraps of cloth, with one of them wrapped around our shoulders and another coiled around our feet. Through some holes, as it were, he could see old man Sage beside him, but the patches of fog would shift back and conceal him. They were light, fragrant, silvery and bracing on his hands and on the skin of his cheeks; they would become transparent in the sun, then, in a gilded ray of sunlight, they formed a thousand tiny drops. Perhaps that is what liberty is, he thinks; and that is what pleasure is, for suddenly a rift appeared over towards the void and there, directly in front of him, at the same height, in the blue, he saw the glaciers shining.

But then he had started making coins... And the candle's flame was sagging now and about to go out. Ah, if only I could have everything, thought Farinet. But, on the contrary, I have to make a choice: either go on living the way I do, or turn myself in. Only that would mean at least six months of being deprived of the outdoors, of being deprived of fresh air and the things that go with it: a dewy leaf, a blade of grass with its pearls, a sprig of red berries to put in my hat; six months and then... And maybe, after all, that's not too high a price to pay for what I could have afterwards, once I've seen her coming, all graceful and shapely, with her caraco like the sky and her slender hen's neck...

At this moment the candle's flame wavered and flared brightly, the wick having suddenly slumped into a pool of molten tallow.

He raised his head and looked all around him.

There was a hole in the ceiling; that is what he sees. By the door, the down mattress, tossed to the floor, had been ripped apart and was spilling its feathers.

He sees how they are treating him; he said aloud, "Never!"

He sees a broken chair, he sees them tramping through plaster.

He rises and grabs his rifle. "Me, turn myself in! Just let them come and get me! ..."

Meanwhile the candle goes out, and he bumps into all sorts of objects and things strewn around the floor as he searches for the door. "Farewell, Romailler."

This is how he is. He gropes his way across the kitchen.

And the first time he takes aim at the moon, it makes him laugh.

He aims at the moon with his number 4 lead and fires the shot…

"Do you hear me or not? Hey, down there! You, the sound sleepers! This means no the first time."

The sound tumbles down the slopes like the pins in a game of ninepins.

"You didn't hear me? Well, then, one more time!"

Bang!

And for a long time the sound rolls down the mountainside like that of a rock slide.

X

They didn't see him again in the village for more than three weeks. Where they did see him, during this time, was up among the chalets high in the mountains, because he ran to and fro there.

On the first day, they had caught sight of him in Pralovin, where he arrived at the same time as the sun, which rendered him pink all over in front of the master, who was gray on his doorstep.

He said to the master, "I couldn't stand it any longer in my hole."

The master said to him, "Are you the one who fired the shots last night?"

"No, not me."

"That's funny."

Then Farinet asked, "The gendarmes, did they come back?"

"Not a one," said the master.

Thus, they engaged in a rather strange conversation that morning. Farinet went on, "It looks like the gendarmes have had enough of me. That's suits me fine. Are there any wild goats[7] up your way?"

"Here and there," said the master. "I haven't seen a lot this year."

At that, Farinet sat down on the bench in front of the chalet.

"Do you have what I need to clean my rifle with?"

"The light's good," he said. I'll point it at the sun."

The master brought him a jar of grease, a ramrod and some rags. Farinet pointed the small end of the barrel at the center of the star, thereby allowing its light to enter and play, evenly distributed, along the whole length of the steel tube.

"Just as I thought, it's a bit pitted. It's damp in that cave."

And, having dipped the rag in grease, he worked it up and down in the barrel with his arm.[8]

"Well, we'll see what that gives us... So long!"

He didn't even want to accept a glass of *fendant* the master offered to him.

Here's the account of the three weeks that Farinet spent running around the mountains. They saw him in Marquisaz, in La Ruinette and in Praz-Pourri.

They also saw him more to the east, in Cherpifou — wherever there are these grassy terraces suspended like balconies painted green high up between the rocks and the snows. They are a few hundred meters long and a hundred meters wide, with twenty, thirty, fifty head of livestock, together with a stone cabin and four or five men who guard the animals and make the butter and cheese — all suspended two thousand to two thousand five hundred meters above the townsmen and everything else.

They would see Farinet from a distance, coming through the rock fields, and they would burst out laughing.

"Ah, here you are... How are things? C'mon in, we insist."

He would go inside and drink their wine, when they had any.

Everywhere he was well received, because they had a soft spot for him and he wasn't stingy with his coins.

Why was Farinet running around the mountains like this?

But towards the end of the month, the weather turned foul; there were thunderstorms accompanied by heavy rains. It also began to get cold.

Thus it was that, towards the end of the month, he reappeared in Pralovin. He had a beard.

"Ah, it's obvious you aren't coming from town," said the master to him. "Where are you coming from?"

All Farinet did was stretch his arm behind him.

"Well, did you shoot anything?"

He replied, "Not a thing."

He flopped down on the bench, made up of an old board and four posts, which stood next to the door of the chalet. He had a scraggly beard, the brim of his hat drooped over his face, and the cuffs of his jacket's sleeves were fraying.

Now, from this bench you could see the whole valley, but not the village, on account of a rise in the land between you and Mièges. Mièges was out of sight, but otherwise the whole valley was visible, while the men from the chalet were at work all around you.

It was a big pasture, or a pasture bigger than the rest. There were eight men, coming and going, or engaged in washing the tubs beneath a wooden sluice jutting out of an embankment.

All of a sudden Farinet said to the master, "Say, you wouldn't happen to have your telescope handy, would you?"

The master brought out the telescope in its case, which was made of gray fabric and held shut with a piece of string, for he took great care of it. He loosened the string.

"With your permission... I'd like to take a look around over there and try to see something."

Farinet turned around towards the cliff behind him, but he wasn't far enough back.

He said, "I can't see anything from here."

"Of course not," said the master. "But you just have to go down lower."

He was the one who made the suggestion. For his part, Farinet acted as though he were just going along with it.

84

Hence, the master led the way and Farinet followed him, until they reached the very edge of the pasture.

"Here we go," said the master. "From here," he said, "you can see everything in all directions. In front and in back, to right and left, down below and up above…"

He swept his arm around him, and tilted his head back and forth.

And it was true. But Farinet, grasping the telescope, turned around and feigned interest in the grand rocks (the ones called Anzymes).

He holds the telescope in front of his right eye, with the other one closed, but he sees nothing at first. All he can see is a whitish disk sprinkled with strands, as when one looks at a sheet of paper through a magnifying glass.

"You have to pull on the tubes or do the opposite and slide them together," said the master. "It depends on what you're looking at."

Farinet slid the tubes, one inside the other, and the world finally sprang into being. It amused him to remake the world.[9] The world comes to meet him. At first, he aimed towards the Anzymes, this piece of the world standing tall there: the Anzymes, a great wall of rocks, an immense staircase of stone, with the steps green on top and the risers gray. But immediately he says, "No, I don't see any."

He meant wild goats. He continues to scan the length of the mountain range with the telescope.

"Oh," he said, "now I'm in the sky, I've overshot, I'm too high, I see a cloud… Do you see it, a little one, pink all over? . . You could look at the moon with this instrument. Do you ever look at it?"

"Why, of course."

"The stars, too?"

"Them, too."

"Good," he said. "Wait a minute, where am I now?"

And, as if he were unaware of it, he was now going much farther to the right and lowering the end of the instrument towards the valley. They were on the very brink of a promontory that jutted out over it, as if they were standing at the prow of a ship. It was just a matter of turning to the side, and Farinet begins to turn to the side. Then it was as if the telescope were becoming too heavy at the big end, as if it were made of lead at that end. All on its own, it bent down and he yielded to its weight. With this, he drops 1,000 meters, 1,200 meters, 1,500 meters; he drops straight down into the blue hole above a bend in the Rhône, which he sees tossing high and seething like fermenting wine.

But that's not it. He glides, he crawls in the sand among the willow bushes. He is above a plantation of apricot trees packed so close together that they form, as it were, a cobblestone pavement with their rounded tops. He is getting impatient.

He has trouble aiming, because the slightest movement he makes with the big end of the telescope is multiplied a thousand times on the opposite side of the void, there where reality begins again.

Suddenly he finds himself above the village. He sees the rooftops, two-toned because one side is in the shade, while the other is bathed in sunlight; they are made of slate, of broad sheets of slate; they shine like silver on one side, and are as velvety as moleskin on the other.

That's still not it.

All at once, he said to the master, "Could you recognize a person at this distance?"

"Recognize one? No, you can't. Not the individual, but you can tell it's a person. Whether it's a man or a woman, sure. If it's a gendarme, for example... What are you looking for?"

"Nothing."

Farinet is still concentrating, now barely moving the tube, which he holds gripped tightly in his hands. And then — that's it!

Yes, that's it. A little house, brand-new. He sees the roof; he sees the base of the walls, the flowers in the garden, the China asters, some pink, some yellow, some blue. But there is no one in the garden.

"Whew," he says. "This is tiring. I need to take a rest."

He lowers the telescope.

"Yes, that tires the wrist."

"You think so?"

"Yes, the eye, too. And then the inside of your head…"

XI

The evening that Farinet left, she came as usual with her sack towards ten o'clock. As usual, bending down over the entrance to the passageway, she called out to him, "Tô!" There was no reply.

She calls out a second time, a third time. No reply came back.

She was sad, but not overmuch. "Well," she said to herself, "he can't stay cooped up all the time. He must have gone out for some fresh air. That's natural. I'll wait."

So, after hiding the sack in the barberry bush, she crouched down close by.

She is patient. She tells herself, "He'll come back." She tells herself, "He has a perfect right to go out for a bit," and, after all, she loves him. She just gets up from time to time to call out again, because there was the other entrance that overlooked the gorge, by which he might have come back.

And so the clock in Mièges tolled in the distance, first ten o'clock, then a quarter past, then the half-hour, then three-quarters past. Finally, the eleven strokes wafted to her slowly, one by one, over the desolate pathways of the air, each stroke coughed out separately: one, then another (in no hurry), then yet another (in no hurry)…

She counts. That makes…

My God! . . All at once she rose to her feet.

She set out at a run towards the village. He must have gone out and run into the gendarmes, or they must have hidden themselves behind a tree; maybe he's looking for me, maybe he needs me…

She ran so fast that she was already nearing the first houses. But she sees that everything is peaceful here; everything is the same as it is every evening in the gardens she crosses. She looks at the rows of windows, already darkened, stacked one above the other beneath the eaves (for there were as many as three rows in the façades of the houses).

Crittin had just closed up his place and was about to go upstairs to bed.

She was still out of breath. She asks, "He hasn't come by?"

"No."

"Oh!"

"What about you, you haven't seen him, either?…"

"No… I'll have to go back."

But Crittin got angry.

"See here, you're being foolish. What makes you think anything can happen to him without us knowing about it right away? He must have gone out for a stroll. He can't sit still, that one!"

That is how he spoke, holding his candle in his hand. And perhaps what he said was true, even surely so, she thought — when the two shots rang out, one after the other (when Farinet was firing at the moon), making Crittin freeze in the middle of the staircase.

She turned utterly pale at the foot of the stairs. For a moment, she was unable to breathe, then she wanted to run to the door, but Crittin held her back by the arm.

"Don't move!"

They heard nothing more.

"Let me go!"

"I forbid you…"

He was holding her by her wrists. Then a window opened, followed by another. A voice inquires, "Where is that coming from?"

"Oh, it's real close."

Yet another window opens, and two men talk back and forth across the street, but they are too far away for one to make out what they are saying. Then the window closes again; they have stopped talking. Another window closes...

Nothing more.

Crittin let go of her. He started to laugh, because he had been afraid.

"We're being silly," he said. "He must have been out hunting. He was shooting at a fox."

And as she still wasn't moving, he said, "Go on upstairs first. I'll wait another moment."

She had no choice but to do as he said; she sat down in a chair in her room. She listened. Nothing. Or just — though the windows were closed, and despite how great the silence was, in the farthest reaches of the night — the Rhône. A muffled, intermittent voice, a vast, yet very gentle, breathing that she hears, then hears no more.

The next morning, people came up to one another in the village.

"Did you hear it?"

"Yes, and you?"

"For a moment I was afraid they were shooting at him."

"Bah!" said Fontana. "That's not the sound a carbine makes. He must have been out hunting and shot a fox. (He said the same thing as Crittin.) What do you expect? He has to keep himself alive."

Everyone was of the same opinion, but Joséphine said to herself, "Where is he? Why didn't he tell me he was going out and where he was going?"

For, the next day, she went back to the cave, and the day after that as well. Then she brought the sack back, because the foodstuffs in it could eventually spoil.

This is Farinet's escape; this is how he managed to get away, and by now he should be up in the mountains, because this is chamois season, said Crittin. But what on earth was he going to do in the mountains? Why was he staying there so long? And the people began to whisper things in each another's ears. "Well," they said, their voices low, "it looks like he's come to an understanding with the law. The proof is that it's been a good two weeks since we last saw a gendarme in the village or hereabouts." There were whispers, because these were not the sort of things to say out loud. Can you believe that he's so attached to freedom? Freedom, what is that? … And then, *afterwards*, he'll be free, free and undisturbed, like the rest of us, no more, no less. And God knows… Maybe for him it's just a matter of pride… He's thinking it over… He has until the end of the month to make up his mind…

That day, a man by the name of Baptiste Rey came into Crittin's place around three o'clock, that is, at the moment when the café is empty, at least at this time of the year, with all the men busy hoeing weeds, mowing or gathering the harvest. But, as for him, he neither hoed, nor mowed, nor gathered.

He came in and ordered a gum syrup.

He was the son of the postal clerk. His job consisted of helping his mother in the post office.

Pale, short, slightly lopsided and hunchbacked, with a bad complexion, a hangdog look — he said he couldn't stand wine, which is why he ordered a gum syrup.

Despite all that, he had a reputation as a ladies' man. People said he had tried to pay court to Romailler's daughter.

He made no noise; he was dropping by, neighbor to neighbor. He had on slippers. He had on a linen vest. He had no jacket. Joséphine hadn't heard him come in. She was knitting, all alone in the kitchen by the open window. As for Crittin, he always went to take a nap every day from one to three o'clock.

Baptiste must have known this. So he took his sweet time, walking along the walls and reading the official (and unofficial) announcements posted on them. Beneath the cantonal seal with its stars and a river, he read:

Notice. Decree. Hunting Regulations. Taxes. Elections on the — th of September...

Beneath the seal of a free country and printed in beautiful, thick, black type with the title in capital letters, on a large-format sheet of white paper.

He made no sound in his slippers, as he went along beneath the seals with his hands in his pockets. The seals are divided in half by a vertical line. On one side of the line there are stars that are for the districts; on the other side, a few wavy, horizontal lines represent a watercourse that is a river, that is our Rhône.[10]

A rather scantily dressed lady was holding a bunch of grapes beneath some medallions. A pretty, little, round breast—which Rey, taking a seat, keeps staring at—is left uncovered by a tiger skin thrown over the opposite shoulder.

"Hey, anybody here?"

Again he says, "Hey!"

"Good afternoon, Mademoiselle Joséphine... A gum syrup and some water, nice and cool. There's a storm coming; that works up a thirst."

She stood before him, fully dressed and not so pleasing to the eye. She said nothing. He sees this large face, a bit sad with freckles on dark skin. She has on a cotton caraco, black with white polka dots, that hangs down around her hips. A high collar and long sleeves.

Ah, not so appealing as the lady on the poster that he is examining once again (Joséphine had gone out). "Aagh! Farinet, a bit too short, a bit too robust, wouldn't you say?" Baptiste said to himself. "And then maybe not so young anymore, with her hair pulled back too much, eh? too tight and too thin in the back" — while the other one, with her arm raised, has her hair undone and curling over her forehead, while, more to the sides, it is draped over her beautiful, smooth, white skin.

Joséphine had come back. She set a glass half-filled with a yellow liquid on the table, as well as a jug filled with water and covered with condensation.

"Thank you very much."

Then, as he sees her about to go back, he says, "How are you doing, Mademoiselle Joséphine?"

"Not bad, thank you. And you?"

"Not bad."

She was still standing just a few steps from him, and half turned away. He isn't looking at her, or scarcely so. As he pours the water from the jug into the glass, where the mixture becomes cloudy and pale, he asks, "Is there something wrong? It looks kind of lonely here. You don't get a lot of business this time of year, do you?"

"Not so much, obviously," she said. "People are too busy."

Finally, she turned around to face him. Her hands were clasped in front of her stiff linen apron with its thin stripes of violet and black.

"Well," he said, "I can see that. It's a bit dull."

He raises his glass and takes a swig of gum syrup.

"That does me good…"

After a pause, he asks, "Have you had any news?"

"News? News about who?"

"Oh, you know who…"

At that, she froze. However, her dark face may have become a shade darker; her big hands are dangling. There behind her is the lady holding a bunch of grapes.

"Ah, yes," he says. "It's like that."

He drinks another mouthful of syrup. A blue fly circled his glass.

And suddenly he comes out with, "You wouldn't know whether what they say is true, would you?"

"What do they say?"

"Oh, well, if you don't know... Maybe it's just idle talk."

"And just what is this idle talk?"

"Well, then, since you asked," he went on. "There are those who claim that he's going to turn himself in between now and the end of the month."

But she bursts out laughing.

"Whether it's true or not, I have no idea... Be that as it may, he's been to see Romailler."

"When was that?" she said.

"The evening when there were those gunshots, surely you remember them. He hasn't been seen since."

She said nothing more.

"And it just so happens, you see," — he lowers his voice — "Romailler is a councillor, and Romailler is on good terms with these gentlemen from the government..."

He drinks a mouthful of syrup. Her eyes follow the movement of the glass; they are raised with the glass and they drop back down with it.

"Well, they're afraid of the liberals... Only they're also afraid that if they used force, things would get ugly... So...so it would appear that they've instructed Romailler to offer him some propositions..."

He is looking at the lady on the wall. Joséphine's eyes follow his. Then she shrugged.

"Well, he may be telling himself that things can't go on

much longer this way... Another month or two and it'll be winter."

"And then what?" says she.

"Oh!" says he. "Down in a cave! The frosts and the snow..."

He swallowed another mouthful and his glass was empty. He looked at the lady on the wall again.

"And then they say there's also..."

He stands up.

"There's also the fact that Romailler has a daughter, she's eighteen and pretty, and her father has money..."

He was turning his back to Joséphine and heading towards the door.

"Well, isn't that so? That counts for something. Those things count for something, too. Good-bye, Mademoiselle Joséphine..."

All this time she hasn't budged, and he pads away in his slippers. She sees his hump and his crooked body; she sees him from behind; she sees him reaching the door and about to open it.

"It's not true! ...Liar! ..."

And he goes out, but he is still not yet out the door.

"Coward!"

Again, louder so he can hear it.

"Coward!"

The lady holding a bunch of grapes is on the wall, and pleasing to the eye. There is a blue fly, and many black ones.

She held the kerosene lamp raised above her head and said to herself, "Maybe I'm not beautiful enough anymore, maybe I'm not young enough anymore for him."

It was a lamp having a glass reservoir and a weld-metal base, together with a shabby cardboard lampshade fraying at the edges. But everything was wretched and old in this room, including the mirror, which was an abject and cheap little thing in an iron frame painted to look like wood, with its glass full of defects that gave you one eye higher than the other, a crooked nose and a lump in the middle of your cheek.

Rey kept looking at the lady holding a bunch of grapes; Rey was making comparisons. And what about *him?* Couldn't he have done the same thing?

Maybe he's had enough of me!

She tries to put her thoughts in order. For the past few days, it seemed to her that the regulars in the café would lower their voices when she made as if to approach them. She pictures Ardèvaz, she pictures Fontana; they seemed to be embarrassed in her presence — or is she imagining things? She thinks, "But the gendarmes, too — it's true we haven't seen a single one since Farinet took off, it's going on three weeks. What does that prove? ..." She tells herself that perhaps it doesn't prove a thing. Only now there's what Rey told her. And this daughter of Romailler's, it's true that she's pretty; maybe that's why they talk low when I'm around. Maybe they know things that even Rey himself doesn't know. She's pretty. She's pretty and young, and they say she's pleasant and has a good character, and she's a hard worker. And me? ...

She looks at herself, again raising the lamp above her head. Then she starts to laugh. Young and pretty, it's true, but what does that prove? ...That's why she laughs... After all, Farinet isn't crazy enough to think that Romailler would give him his daughter... A man who's been in prison! ... A man who ought to be there still! ... A man who is forced to hide underground like a grub worm... A man who would have been caught again a long time ago, if he hadn't met me... Because there's me! She laughs. There's me, there's me! After all, he's not so stupid as to think that Romailler, who is rich, who is a councillor, who is highly respected… and besides, I'm here. She laughs again. It's all Rey's doing, because lies don't embarrass him. He had his sights set on the girl and he wanted to take his revenge… As for *him,* well, he'll come back and then I'll have a talk with him. I'll say to him, "Why did you leave without saying a word to me, Farinet, king of the heartless? Are you tired of me?" And once again raising the lamp, she says to herself, "Let's see, how old is he? And me?" He's twenty-seven years old and I'm thirty. The thing is, other women also have ways of making themselves look more attractive, things for straightening their hair, things like raspberry syrup, money… As for me…

She set the lamp on the table.

She unhooks the mirror, which is hanging from a nail. Midnight chimes.

She still can't see anything in it, so she raises the wick in the lamp and removes the shade.

Setting the mirror at an angle on the little deal table that serves her as a dressing table, she examines herself closely.

She has on a stiff, coarse linen blouse, with half-length sleeves, that reaches up to her neck.

Not beautiful enough for him anymore?

Only she sees the line that she has around her neck like a necklace, and her neck is brown above the line and white below it.

She sees this same line, a little above her elbows, that divides her arms in two.

And then there is, on her right breast, in place of the pretty pink tip, an ugly brownish mark in the bottom of the mirror, like those that people call *coffee stains.*

XII

Just three days later — that is to say, on August 30th — some little girls, who had been out gathering blackberries above the village, came back saying that they had seen him.

"Who?"

"Farinet."

"Where?"

"At the bottom of the stones."

Between the place where the great rocks end and the one where the meadows begin, there is a narrow scree field occupied by pines and edged with brambles. That is where, they said, he had suddenly shown up.

"Are you quite sure it was him?"

"Oh, yes!"

It was the thirtieth of August (which has thirty-one days).

"Did he say anything to you?"

"No."

"Then what?"

"Oh, we didn't dare stay."

That is what the little girls said when they came down to the village around five o'clock with their pails only half full. They were telling the truth.

He was coming down from the mountains.

He must have taken a shortcut through the scree field and dropped straight down to a point he had decided on beforehand. This is where he had appeared, abruptly shoving apart the lower branches of a hazelnut tree. He had flopped down to sit on top of the scree; meanwhile, the little girls fled, their wooden soles clattering and their pails banging together.

It is beginning — or it is beginning anew. Farinet was still steaming a little, because it was hot out. It had rained until noon, then the weather had cleared. He is giving off steam in his coarse, brown-wool garments, on which there were dark spots where they were still damp and other spots that were nearly gray. One can see that he has a knapsack on his back. The brim of his hat hangs down on one side, exposing a swath of hair and the top of the ear.

That day, the clouds, yielding little by little to their weight in the motionless air, had slid down the mountain slopes much lower than the boulders and the forests; that day, a dismal light was evenly spread everywhere. That day, there reigned a vast silence beneath the low sky. Someone is hammering a nail, then all is quiet; someone is driving a nail home somewhere with the back of a hatchet. Someone is scraping away in his vineyard. Farinet gives off white smoke. He is motionless. Today — one more day to go.

For now he has come back. He sees that he has been led back. Now he sees, quite close by, between his upraised knees, the garden fence, the new little house and the flowers in their beds of well-watered soil. The zinnias are yellow, pink or even deep red. He sees the dahlia bushes; he moves one of his knees and the dahlias are no longer there. He moves the other knee and instantly does away with the multicolored zinnias, neatly aligned in their bed below him. He was still steaming; he was nearly done steaming. Someone in the village was banging again on a plank. Farinet is still motionless, and there is no longer anything in the garden, nor anywhere around him, except a tiny train out on the plain, with its thick white smoke stretching out more and more. What should he do? Suddenly, he said to himself, "After all…" At least, that is what he must have said. Then he removes the pack from his back and one can see that there is something inside it. He sets his rifle down next to him and, holding the pack between his knees, he untied the cord that keeps it shut. After all, this doesn't commit him to anything. It's just a gift, he says to himself. He sees that the gift is still there, gone quite stiff and cold. He closes the pack again. It's high time I repaid Romailler for his courtesy. He takes another look; he sees that there is still no one in the garden and that the door to the house remains closed. He slings his pack over his left shoulder, and his rifle over his right shoulder.

It was at this moment that the little girls announced the news about him to the village.

He descended so quickly that he was quite surprised to see that he had arrived. Romailler's house was next to him, as if it had been built much higher up on the slope. It is here; he sees its blue shutters and the unpainted wooden fence enclosing the garden — and he sees that the gate is wide open. Yet he stopped short. Then he moves forward; then he stops. Then he moves forward again and finds himself brought in this way to the foot of the steps leading to the front porch.

Here he stops again.

He doesn't mount the steps. He listens to hear whether anyone has heard him, whether anyone was coming. Then, all at once, he calls out, "Anyone here? Hey!"

And one more time, "Hey!"

At that, inside the house, there was the noise of a chair being pushed back. The door at the top of the steps opened. He still couldn't see anyone from where he was.

And it wasn't Romailler, for now the person was coming out onto the porch. He removed his hat.

"Oh, pardon me, Mademoiselle."

She was holding a piece of sewing. She did not recognize him at first, then she turned quite pink above her caraco the color of the sky.

"Oh, it's you, Monsieur Farinet."

"Is your father here?"

"No."

He is at the bottom of the steps; she is at the top of the steps.

"No," she said, "he had an appointment in the village, but he may be back soon. Would you like to wait for him a little while?"

He says no.

"Oh, Monsieur Farinet," she goes on, "is it true?…"

Emboldened by distance, she went on, "Wouldn't you like to come in?"

After all, perhaps he is hungry or thirsty. But he said no, what for? He doesn't budge from where he is; he indicates by a gesture that he doesn't want to come in.

"Well…well, some other time," he said abruptly.

"That's too bad. Oh! Monsieur Farinet…"

"Listen…"

He stops.

"Mademoiselle…I had something here… For you."

"What? For me…"

"Oh! It's not very big…"

He sets his rifle against the wall and removes the pack from his back, while she watches him from the top of the steps.

Opening the pack, he said, "It weighs around five or six pounds. It's not much, but they're kind of scrawny up there…"

He pulls a small hare from his pack and holds it up by its hind legs. A drop of blood runs down the animal's neck to form a pearl at the tip of its muzzle.

"Oh! Monsieur Farinet... Did you shoot it yourself?"

He makes no reply.

"Is it for me? Oh! Thank you very much..."

And he too stood motionless, with his arm bent, holding the animal in front of him by the two paws: a wretched little hare of the mountains, stiff as a board, as if it had been whittled out of a piece of wood with a bit of tow glued on top. Then she saw that he was handsome.

And tall and strong (he was holding his hare), yet wild, with his two-week-old beard, his unkempt hair, his face sunburned red over his dark skin tone, and his deep-blue eyes that seem to gaze from two holes...

They gaze at her, and she — all of a sudden she runs down the steps, stops, holds out her hand, dares not and draws it back; she no longer dares even to look at him, so she lowers her head...

"Oh!" he said then. "Is it true?"

He no longer quite knows what he is saying.

"Listen," he said.

She took the animal. He was closing his pack and fumbling for words now.

"Listen, I'll come back... Would you tell your father...yes, that I'll come back tomorrow... Yes, tomorrow evening, around...around nine o'clock..."

He said, "Well, good-bye then, Mademoiselle."

He puts his hat back on his head; he goes away; he leaves the garden.

However, he can't help turning around once he has reached the path; he sees that she hasn't left her place.

She must have followed him with her eyes, because as soon as he has turned around, their eyes meet.

And, still farther away, he turns around one more time. She is still there, faithfully following him with her gaze.

Then he said to himself, "Things are going well!"

Why does he say to himself, "Things are going well," as he vigorously inhales the sad, moist air, which yet becomes fresh and thirst-quenching, as when one is parched and one swallows a glassful of water? The weather is new; the year is new; the day is new. Everything shines around him, where before it was dull.

He sees some people and goes towards them.

They were astonished to see that he was no longer in hiding and that, instead of making a detour through places that were out of the way, here he was coming straight down towards the village.

"Hey! Lavallaz," he said. "How are you?"

This to a young man weeding in his vineyard.

"I'm fine. And you?"

"Me too. How's the vineyard?"

"Not too bad."

He had already gone past. Meanwhile, the other man, who had replied without thinking, recovered little by little from his surprise. With his hands on the handle of his spade, he said to himself, "Why, it's Farinet..."

"Yes, it's him... You're seeing him, all right... Well," said Farinet, "Father Cranche, it's steep as ever around here. Even a little too much, wouldn't you say?"[11]

This time he stopped. With difficulty, the old man straightened himself up, putting his left hand on the small of his back, which made cracking noises.

"Huh? What?... Oh, Lord ha' mercy! It's Farinet! Where's he coming from?"

"Of course, it's Farinet…"

"Hey, watch out," Cranche started to say…

But Farinet had already passed on, going over to a woman who was working in her vegetable garden. They could see her headscarf, black with red flowers, fluttering with joy among the beanpoles.

XIII

"Ah, it's you! Ah, here you are…"

It is him speaking.

She sees that he is cheerful and he is laughing.

"You've brought me something to drink and eat. It couldn't come at a better time… You're a good girl… But be quick about it, I'm in a hurry."

Farinet sat down on the edge of his straw mattress in the cave. Josephine passes him the bread (it was a large, flat loaf of rye). Next, she passed him, carefully wrapped in paper, the first pears of the season.

"This couldn't be better! Here I've been on bread and water for more than three weeks, most often just on water alone. What time is it?"

She said, "Nine o'clock."

"Well, then, I haven't eaten anything since ten o'clock this morning. You know, that's a long time."

In high spirits and ravenous, he cut into the loaf and stabbed the slices of dried meat with the tip of his knife.

"Three weeks and more, that adds up! … And pour me a drink while you're at it."

She filled the glass.

"Thanks… Your health!"

He drained it in one go.

"Another one."

No sooner was it filled than he empties the glass again.

"Good things come in threes… Another one."

He empties it likewise.

Then he goes back to eating.

"So, how are things?"

Taken aback, she made no reply. She gazes at him. All she sees is that he is there. When the little girls announced that they had seen him, she had been happy. Is she still happy?

She is surprised at his good mood and his air of contentment. She is happy to see him content; she is troubled to see him content.

For his part, he didn't even wait for her reply.

"Me, things are fine... In any case, they're better. I had a hole in my stomach, a hole more than three weeks in the making..."

This is when she started in.

"Oh, Farinet, why didn't you tell me anything? Why did you leave without saying a word to me? ..."

"Ah!" he said. "It wasn't possible."

"Why not? ... I came, and you weren't here. I came again, and you weren't here. And I came one more time and you still weren't here..."

"That's true..."

He is being reasonable and calm, as she can see.

"What you're saying is true, but, you see, in my situation..."

"That's just it, in your situation... Listen..."

She interrupted him, then she interrupts herself, while he — with the knife in one hand and a hunk of bread in the other — he stops cutting into his bread.

For he saw clearly that she was coming to the point. And, indeed, now she said, "It's a good thing you've come back, because we have to leave now."

Taken by surprise, he started to laugh and then said, in a joking way, "When would that be?"

She can see that he is in a joking mood, and it lacerates her heart.

"This is serious," she said. "Right now," she said. "This evening."

But he went back to eating.

"Yes," she went on. "You can't stay here any longer. This can't go on… Do you think the gendarmes won't come here looking for you in the end, if they can't get you any other way? They know very well where you're hidden, only they'd rather not pay too high a price to get you, so they're biding their time. But they won't wait forever," she said. "And then there's the winter. Winter's coming. What are you going to do in your cave? Will you be able to keep on chasing around the mountains when the flocks have come down? Answer me that! And they will come down. And what about when the snow will be spread, up there in the high places, wherever it can stick, like nasty moss on the trees? Then, if you go out, the gendarmes… If you stay in hiding: illness, the cold, the stale air, I don't know. Listen…"

But he said, "Are you finished?"

He is still calm, and still in a joking mood.

"And where would we go, Joséphine?"

"We would go far away."

"Far away. And where's that?"

"I don't know, we could cross the border, because the gendarmes can't. We'd have to start a new life. I don't know, in Evian, in Geneva… But far, far, far away," she went on. "Please, can't you see? Far from here, and right this minute, Farinet…"

She said, "That's it." She bows her head.

"As for me, I don't know, but I feel sad. I don't know, Farinet, but I'm afraid."

To which, he said only, "And what about money?"

"Do you have any?"

"No."

"Oh, Farinet. How can you dare to say that?…"

"That's just like a woman, she mixes everything up. I don't have any money at all," he says. "All I have is gold… Gold — I have as much of that as you want, in powder and coins…"

He gets up.

"Here."

He holds out to her the little box that he has just picked up from the projecting slab that serves as his workbench.

"It's full… Well, do you know what it's worth? It's worthless. It's worthless in the eyes of the government. You know very well it is… It's too beautiful. It's worth more than their gold and that's why I'm here. You know very well this is so, but you don't think it through, you're just like all women…"

Then he laughed again, but with a twinge of pain.

"Just you try to use it, you'll see what happens. It hasn't worked out for me. All I can count on are my friends, because they have faith… How about you, do you have faith? Well, then," he said, "take it, it's yours. I'm giving it to you…"

He held the box out to her, but she recoils, putting her hands behind her back.

"Oh! Farinet."

And, still standing, she takes another step backward, which brought her right up against the cave wall.

"Oh! Farinet, is it true then? …"

"Is what true?"

She can see that he is losing his self-assurance and his voice is becoming unsteady.

"What people are saying."

"What are people saying?"

"Ah! You know very well."

"No… I don't know."

"They say you're going to turn yourself in… And Romailler has a daughter. Maurice, tell me, is it true?"

At this, he said nothing in reply.

And she — she places her hand flat against her cheek as one does when one has a toothache. He wanted to say something, but she shakes her head slowly from right to left, from left to right, over and over.

"So what's to become of me? Maurice, me, huh? All alone… Huh? Maurice, if you make a deal with the authorities, if you go away, and me not pretty anymore, huh? Maurice, and not that young anymore… And then what people are saying…"

"Listen, c'mon now…"

But then his arm drops down to his side, while she draws herself up.

"You miserable… No, don't come near me! I forbid you… You deceived me! You took advantage of me when you needed me, and now… No…no… Oh! I see through you now…"

And her voice grows low and monotone, as when one recites from a book at school.

"That's how it goes. They're glad to have you around, when they have no one else to turn to. You go along with it, you don't get it, you think they're fond of you… Yes, I remember it well… It's not ancient history…Where was it you'd just come from?" she asked. "Ah! You were in a tight spot and at wits' end, that morning back in Sion! You don't remember — it's easier that way — that morning…"

Still at a loss for something to say, he shrugged his shoulders, as when one resigns oneself to something that can't be helped.

"Who was always the first one up? And I had to wait on customers and sweep the café, not like some of these young ladies... Oh! Just say it. Hey! Say it, I don't mind. Yet you were quite happy that I was there, otherwise what would you have done, without a penny, tell me, without papers? ..."

"I thank you," she went on. "Hey, he paid me with one of his coins, can you believe it? He thought I wouldn't notice a thing. Ah! My poor friend! But what a fool I was! Ah! what a fool I was! 'Cause what did I do? I went to my room to get my money, and the change I gave him was my own money, because I wanted to keep his coin..."

"Joséphine!"

"No," she said. "I'm talking, let me talk. I haven't finished. I have too many things to get off my chest. They're weighing me down... And I have the time, you know. I have lots of time, all the time I want... Because you're not leaving here without my say-so. Ah! You thought you were? ... *Monsieur* Farinet," she says (and she gives him a strange look), "because you are a *monsieur*... Well, then, *Monsieur* Farinet, if it weren't for me... Ah! I was a fool... If it weren't for me, you'd still be in the *galleys*, right? Still in yellow pants with a black stripe, looking a bit conspicuous. And still with a gendarme beside you, with a loaded gun, right? ... 'Cause they'll make you sweep the streets and they're afraid you'll run off... Well, me, I looked at you and I thought, "The poor wretches!" Ah! I was a fool... If it weren't for me..."

She stopped short and said, "Is this true or not?"

"It's true."

"Ah! You do see... Next, you're going to tell me... Who was it who smuggled the file to you? It was me, wasn't it? ..."

"C'mon, Joséphine."

"Answer me."

"Yes, you."

"Good," she said. "And who arranged things with the guards so that they didn't search me when I brought you the rope? And who made an agreement with Crittin later on, and—ever the servant—ended up both his servant and (alas!) yours? Answer me."

And meekly, he replied, "It's true. It's you."

"Then, when you got out of the *galleys*, who rose early every day and didn't go to bed till after midnight, because she had to feed you and come to see you... Is it true, what I'm saying? I had to come myself at night, each night crawling in the dark, so that nobody would see me. And on account of who? Answer me!"

"Oh!" he says.

"And carrying a load. Oh, a heavy load, and on account of who?"

"Listen, Joséphine..."

"Answer me," she says. "Answer. Say 'It's on account of me.'"

"It's on account of me, that's true..."

"Well, then, in that case, we're going to leave. As for you, you have everything you need right here. I'll go and pack my suitcase. We'll leave this very night..."

In the brief silence that ensued they could hear the whispering of the water down in the gorge, and there was time enough for a drop to fall from the vaulted ceiling and splatter on the floor with a sharp snap, as when a match is struck.

Then he begins to speak, or tried to begin, saying, "Oh! I know full well."

He hesitates.

"Oh, you're a good girl—I know full well you are— both devoted and a hard worker and all, but…"

"But what?"

"It's impossible."

At that, all she said was, "Oh!"

Then once again she started to back away a little, then she said, "Oh! Maurice."

Then her gaze became remote; it withdrew inside her. Then, suddenly reappearing, it wanders about as if it had no idea where to rest itself.

"That?" she said all of a sudden.

It was the little box full of coins that Farinet had set next to him on the mattress.

"That," she said, a little dreamily, "that, it would be mine, then? …"

"Of course, I already told you so."

"I can take it?"

He became cheerful and happy again.

"Of course, you can… Here!"

He holds it out to her. No sooner did she take it, than she turned her back on him.

He looks; she is no longer there. He only hears her footsteps as they recede in the unlighted stretch of the passageway.

He called out, "Hey, where're you going?"

He goes to get the light.

"Wait, I'm coming with the light… Wait, you'll hurt your-self…"

He rushes after her in the narrow passage where she already has a head start.

"Wait, I don't know whether the ladder's in place."

He reaches the ladder. It was still moving…

XIV

Then, the next morning, Romailler made sure he went to the mayor's house early, so as to catch him still at home. This was towards seven o'clock, even a little before seven. It was a fine day. The weather had cleared overnight, and the heavy fog that blanketed the mountainsides the evening before had turned into delicate veils, transparent and white, which could be seen rising on all sides towards a freshly repainted sky.

The two men sat down in front of the house beneath a vine arbor on which the grapes were beginning to ripen, so that the dangling clusters were of two colors, with some grapes green and others pink or light violet. This was at the top of the lane that ran down to the village's only street. Beneath the clusters of grapes of two colors, they sat down against the whitewashed foundation and were faced towards the east. Overlooking the other houses, they had before them a sweeping view of the great valley.

They were paying no attention to it, but occasionally they chanced to raise their heads, at which the sun, up above, would dart its shaft through a rent in the clouds straight into their eyes. It would already be half hidden again by the time one of the men (or the two of them at once), in the air both warm and chilly — chilly up to their knees or their bellies, warm around their heads and shoulders — would hurriedly pull the brim of his hat down in front.

Ah, it is a fine bowman!

The sun appeared suddenly, then it disappeared. It lets fly with its shafts. They strike, with their hard points, the slate tiles on the rooftops. And from time to time, a man with a pannier on his back would pass by, on his way up to his vineyard.

"...so I came right over to inform you," said Romailler, "because there may be some arrangements to make."

"Yes," said the mayor.

At that moment, two little girls belonging to a neighbor appeared on the doorstep; both wore woolen shawls crossed over their chests, and each was nibbling on a thick slice of buttered bread topped with honey.

"My daughter is the one who received him," Romailler went on. "He asked her to let me know that he would come back this evening, around nine o'clock. Today's the thirty-first, and I had told him he had until the thirty-first."

"Well, then," said the mayor, "it's clear he's turning himself in…"

"So it seems to me, but if he is turning himself in, what shall we do with him, while the authorities are being notified?"

"You'll have to keep him at your place, if you can."

"Oh, I could…"

"Good. Then you make him sign a document, so that everything is in order and we are covered, in case something should happen. After which, if I were you…"

The mayor went on, "I'd accompany him openly to Sion. You'd take the first train. By sticking to the heights, you wouldn't have to pass through the village. No one would see you. He wouldn't have to suffer the humiliation of being led away by the gendarmes."

"Yes," said Romailler. "And what if he isn't willing?"

"He'll be willing enough, if he comes to see you."

"Oh, he'll come, all right," said Romailler. "He told my daughter so."

"Moreover, he'll see for himself that we're only trying to make things easier for him. But you've given him fair notice of what we expect from him: that he stop making his coins, that he turn over to the authorities all the ones he has left, and that he commit himself to living like the rest of us once he is released…"

CHARLES FERDINAND RAMUZ

The two men talked quietly. The mother of the two little girls just called them over to remove their shawls. And the great clouds kept rising before the mountains, in their transparent robes whose loose fabric was fraying, then disappearing little by little. The sun was stripped bare; it could no longer be looked at.

By now the mayor's feet had warmed up, as had Romailler's. Suddenly the mayor spoke up again.

"The hitch is that woman. Have you spoken to him about her?"

Romailler shook his head.

"Well, then, he'll also have to commit himself to marrying her... He can't go on living this way, nor can she. It doesn't look right. Especially if he comes back to live in the village. You'll have to bring it up..."

Romailler looked embarrassed, and didn't reply right away. Just then, another man was making his way up to his vineyard with his pannier, from which protruded the end of the handle of some tool...

Someone gives a shout in the distance.

"Baptiste!"

Then they heard more shouting in the distance.

"Baptiste! ... Baptiste! ..."

The man with the pannier turns towards Romailler and the mayor.

"What's going on?"

They say nothing in reply; they stand up and come out onto the lane.

Then, down at the far end of it, they see a woman running, then another one, then another woman has appeared at her window.

"Come quick! Come quick! Baptiste! Ah, my God!"

116

A woman's voice, quite shrill. It too is coming from the street, over the rooftops, a little to the right of the lane.

At this moment, a man appears in the opening at the end of the lane. He stops there and looks toward the mayor's house, which isn't far away. Suddenly, he spots the mayor himself, standing with Romailler in the middle of the lane.

He merely raises his arm, by way of beckoning them to come.

People were coming from all directions and there was already a crowd gathered in the street when the two men arrived in turn.

Crittin was there. Crittin said to them, "Quick, come and see… He must have gone crazy."

"Who?"

"Farinet."

They fail to understand, but they can see that the crowd has formed a little farther along, in front of the post office building. It is a blue building with half of its facing fallen off; though three stories high, it is narrow and has only three windows in its façade. At the street level, there is a sort of store front, which serves as the post office, and a bench where Madame Rey, the postal clerk, sits regularly.

In fact, she is there now. When they arrive, the mayor and Romailler see that she has flopped down on the bench and two women at her side are talking to her.

The men say, "What's the matter?"

She says nothing in response; she shakes her head.

"Ah, someone robbed her last night," says one of the women.

"Yes," says the other, "and how much was it?"

"Eight hundred francs," says Madame Rey, "eight hundred…"

Then all of a sudden, she shouts again, "Baptiste!"

"Yes," she says, "eight hundred francs in beautiful, hundred-franc and fifty-franc notes that were in the drawer. A little while ago, I came down and the drawer was just as I'd left it, locked with a key. I open it… Well, he came during the night and took them from me…"

She screamed, "It's him! Yes, it's him…Farinet… He left his gold in place of them."

At this point, Baptiste finally arrives.

"Go and show them. I can't. I can't move another inch. It's my heart. You'll see, they're his coins, all right. And the government says they're worthless and won't accept them. My God!"

They brought her a small glass of aged *marc*.

Meanwhile the mayor directed the onlookers to step back, then went inside the office with Romailler and Baptiste. The room was divided in two by a wooden partition furnished with a service counter and a door that stood open. The men passed through the door and entered the part of the office closed to the public.

And Baptiste said, "You see? Ah, the bastard…"

He was pointing at the till, wide open with its tin tray filled with yellow coins, dazzling, a little too bright. Then he lifts it (the tray) and there was nothing underneath.

Not one note, not a single silver or copper coin— but all the gold a person could want. Farinet must have counted the money (they knew him well) and scrupulously replaced the sum he took with the same amount in his gold…

"Ah, the pig," Baptiste went on. "The notes…"

"Leave that alone," said the mayor. "Don't touch anything… And run and get me the bailiff."

Then he turns the key in the lock, because there were more and more people in the street, where they went on talking and arguing. Some of them said to Madame Rey, "After all, you have his gold in return…"

"Oh," said one, "that's not the same thing! It's not legal tender, you know..."

"Folks'll buy it from you," said someone to Madame Rey. "I, for one, would be happy to..."

"Hey, watch out now. That's prohibited and the authorities'll step in..."

"All the same, he's not a thief," said one. "I'm sure the money's all there."

"Yes," said someone, "he's an honest fellow."

"He must have needed money. He came to make the swap."

But they stepped aside to make way for the bailiff, who doubled as a rural policeman.

Madame Rey was helped upstairs to her living quarters, because she resided on the third floor.

Some volunteers, including Crittin, were deputized to keep order. Baptiste came back with the bailiff, who banged on the door to the post office (that's how these things are done).

"It's me."

He finds the mayor in the middle of counting the coins. The mayor said, "Forty-two, forty-two at twenty francs each... It's all there."

Then, addressing the bailiff, he says, "You, run over and alert the gendarmerie."

To Baptiste he says, "You, stay here for the investigation."

Romailler said not a word.

The café was full of people. Joséphine went back and forth, waiting on them. She hadn't spoken a word. They called out to her and gave her their orders. She seemed oblivious to whatever else was being said; she took no part in the conversations in full swing at all the tables — for all, or nearly all, of the men in the village had wound up being there. It was now ten o'clock in the morning. When the news reached them, one by one, as they were working in their gardens or in their fields, the men had come, saying to themselves, "Things have taken an ugly turn."

Crittin shook his head gloomily, repeating once again, "He must have gone crazy."

They said to him, "You think so?"

Fontana, seated at a table with Ardèvaz, said nothing.

"You may think so," someone said to Crittin. "It could be just the opposite…"

For, indeed, the general view was that he must have decided to leave the country, so he saw the need to exchange his gold for something that was legal tender everywhere. By now, they said, he must have made it to the frontier. That's assuming he pulled the trick at midnight. They were happy for him.

As for her, who knows? She seemed above it all. She went back and forth, carrying the bottles of wine and the glasses — business was brisk that morning — in her dark-blue blouse with the high collar. Thus, in the midst of the hubbub, she was indifferent and silent, up to the moment when everyone suddenly rushed to the door. The officers of the law were arriving. The mayor was still in the post office with Baptiste. Romailler must have stayed with them, because he hadn't been seen again. Those in the café had heard the harness bells off in the distance. Saxon, which is the chief town, was just an hour away from Mièges, that is to say, half an hour by carriage. It was eleven-thirty; right on time… It was then that he woke up.

Farinet, in his cave, woke up. He yawns.

The men pressed up against the door of the café in an attempt to see what was happening, but didn't dare show themselves in the street, where stood a kind of open carriage drawn by two horses. The gentlemen of the law, three in number, were inside it, while the bailiff and the gendarmes, who had gotten out at the foot of the hill, only appeared a moment later.

And he, in his cave, yawns. He stretches. The straw mattress crackles beneath his weight like a fire made with bone-dry vine shoots. The gentlemen of the law got out of the carriage, as the mayor stepped forward to meet them. — He is just emerging from his slumber, for he has slept twelve hours straight to make up for being deprived of sleep for more than three weeks, when he would bed down beneath an overhanging rock face or stretch out for an hour or two on the hay in a chalet. That sort of thing runs up an account in your body, as if it were a big book where one column records what you are owed. You have to pay yourself back. He had paid himself back, and then some, as he sees when he checks the time on his watch. He sees that it is a quarter to eleven. Then he lies back again on his mattress and puts his hands behind his head.

In the alcove where he is lying, the light enters only after first being reflected, diminished, from the cave wall. Nevertheless, he can see by the color of the light that the weather has cleared overnight and the sun is out. The light is a pretty yellow color — like that of my nuggets — on the vaulted ceiling above his head, opposite a fissure in the rock. The light is moving; he can see it move. It wavers for a moment, like a candle about to go out, but it doesn't go out. It dims; it revives; it dims anew; it suddenly blazes forth — all because of a branch hanging, with all of its leaves, in front of the cave's entrance, where it sways in the breeze created by the rushing stream. He himself doesn't move, his hands behind his head; he gazes at this color. For it is also that of *her* hair, and all the good things in life are this color, he says to himself: fine and pure, soft and warm, warm to the gaze, soft to the touch. That's it! That settles it! And he was quite content. Then he changes (his hands behind his head). He changes

121

visibly; his expression changes visibly, the way the mountain's vast features do when the sun hides behind a cloud. The thing is, there's her; there's Joséphine. He says to himself, "There's her." He said out loud, "There's her…" Then he gets up, because his peace of mind has been snatched from him. There's the stumbling block — it's her, Joséphine. And the scene from last evening comes back to him, along with what she said, and wasn't she right? Oh, she's a good girl, true enough! And devoted, that's true, too. And what would I have done without her? Now that he has gotten up, he sees that he lacks for nothing, thanks to her. She brings me faithfully everything I need, even more than I need. For he sees, set out on the stone slab, the pears with their upright stalks that she had in her sack last evening: Louise Bonnes, pink on one side and golden on the other, already as ripe and juicy as can be. He sees that he even has coffee and a coffee pot, and that there is always a full supply of wood in the corner, thanks to her, who thinks of it — who thinks of everything I need, as he says to himself while lighting the fire. Matches? I have them. Paper? I have it. He felt like smoking. He sees that in the tin box, nice and dry, there is not just tobacco, but an unopened packet of cigars from the Ferme du Valais, the ones he loves, that is to say, the very strongest kind. He lights one with the match he uses to set fire to the paper in the recess where the hearth is, with a channel for the smoke and a pipe in the channel. And she's the one who thought of that. She arrives with the pipe under her arm and that takes care of that. Meanwhile, he is lighting the paper under the bone-dry pine twigs, still covered with needles, that he has laid out crisscross on top — and this is her doing, for he sees the flame as it rises straight up, nearly smokeless, lively and bright, against the cave wall where it bends back and goes to pieces.

Then he went to fetch water. There is a spring that seeps, a drop at a time, from the rock wall, but she has put a bucket underneath it (she's the one who thought of this).

He just has to plunge the three-legged saucepan into the

bucket, then set it on the fire as he smokes his cigar. Well, then, what now?

It is eleven o'clock. It must be understood that he knew nothing about what was going on in the village.

It must be understood that he is at home here. He believes he is safe here. He still has until the evening to think it over and come to a decision. Meanwhile, the authorities are conducting their search at the post office. Next, they summoned Crittin and questioned him, then Joséphine. Eleven-fifteen; eleven-thirty — the coffee is still trickling down, drop by drop, into the coffee pot next to the fire, while he drinks the first cup. And I have sugar, because she thought of it.

What hasn't she thought of?

He drinks his coffee piping hot, after cutting himself a thick slice of bread from the flat loaf and a piece from the wedge of cheese. But then, all of a sudden, it brightens once again within him, as when the sun unexpectedly emerges, in effect, from behind its cloud. Then, the glaciers turn pink again and the rock regains its beautiful colors — because, after all, she took the coins, and I have none left. For the price of a thousand francs' worth of coins. Well, they mean something to her! So he tells himself... At first, she didn't want them, then she must have changed her mind... Well, then? He relights a cigar. Oh, I owed her that much. If only things can be sorted out this way... She'd have the money. Besides, if they put me back in prison, I won't need her anymore. How long? Six months... That's the hardest part, and agreeing to it is hard, because if I didn't agree, they would have to come and get me, and they'd have no end of trouble. Smoking the whole time, he goes and inspects the two holes for mines he has chiseled into the dry rock. One of them is under the rope ladder, the other farther along, in the passage leading to his house. Both of them, he sees, are intact... Well, then, try and come, you gendarmes, try getting in without my consent. You gendarmes, with your smart uniforms, whatever your rank may be and however many you are — two or ten, or fifty or a hundred — all I have to do is light my fuses (and he checks again to make sure they have stayed nice and dry since he soaked them in sulfur). Well, so I go and say to them, "I'm turning myself in"... Is it possible? Ah, I can see them, they'll be glad... Ah, I can see them. They'll try to hide what they're thinking, but they'll think it nonetheless, and it'll show. "Here you are! Well, then, we got you after all..."

It's impossible.

He checks the time on his watch; he sees that it is already half past noon. Time is passing; he sees that he needs to hurry up and think it over some more, because the evening is fast approaching.

It's the thirty-first, the very last moment.

Once again, he has the entrance to the cave in front of him. The light of the day hangs there like a silver curtain; he goes and parts this curtain so he can pass through.

He is in the bright, white light pouring down on him between the rock walls. At certain times of the day, the sun appears high up there in the narrow slit of sky and for a brief spell reaches the landing, so to speak, in front of the cave entrance. Here he sits down to think.

Beyond is a sheer drop of at least fifty meters.

He need only extend his legs slightly for his feet to stick out beyond the edge, with his back against the rock wall and the lower part of his body dangling in the void. They'd have just as much trouble, the gendarmes would, getting at him from this side, he goes on to think, because they'd have to know their way around the passages and nobody does but me. Just to his left there is a kind of ledge that extends from the landing he is sitting on and runs for awhile along the side of the smooth rock wall until it comes to an abrupt end where the rock juts out. Above him there are a few fir trees clinging to life in the crevices; early in their growth, they bent back towards the light by means of a sharp kink right at the base of their stems. Aside from this, there is nothing but the two rock faces, sheer and barely inclined — for the mountain stream has worked its way down, little by little, through the massif like a saw through a tree trunk, from top to bottom, straight down and deviating neither to the right nor to the left. As a result, there are in truth two streams, as it were — two streams, two small rivers. For him, suspended as he is between the two of them and smoking a cigar, they are of nearly the same importance and the same breadth, one up on high and the other down below. What should he do?[12] When he lifts his head, he can make out, between two straight lines (the brinks of the gorge) a swath of the sky whose current is made visible by a cloud caught up in it; when he lowers his head and juts it forward over his knees, there — at the very bottom, slowly flowing in the same direction, eddying and turning back on itself — is the water: water deep, smooth, transparent and yet black. The sound it makes is a gentle sound, a sound of rustling silk, a continuous sound, such that he can no longer tell whether it is being produced by the clouds up on high brushing the surface of the rock or by the element at the bottom rubbing against the rock wall. What should he do? He throws away his cigar, which has gone out. He opened his wallet. He counted the few coins left there — in all probability, this was prompted by a conversation he is having with himself, on this landing suspended in the air. "Ah!" he said again, "Come, yes, just come!" Casting a glance around him, he wraps his arms around his knees. Then he saw her again — it is she who appeared again, in her caraco like a piece of sky. All at once he says to himself, "Well, then, I'll go. The thirty-first. That's it! I'm going!"

And I'll tell Romailler...

But all the same, I'll have to speak to him — speak to him about her. Do I dare?

Then he sees her smiling at him and saying to him, "You have to dare."

Then a kind of delicate light appears again around his mouth. If *she* will have him... And she will have me, I believe. I've been in prison, but she knows very well why I was there. They're going to put me back there, but that's because I'll let them. After that, I'll be straight with the law, he thinks.

Then the faint light grows stronger in the midst of his short beard... I'll have paid my debt and they'll leave me in peace. And Joséphine'll have the money...

I'll go back to work in the vineyards. Romailler has some property; this'll save him the expense of one worker...

And then I'll go and see Paltani, the stonemason, 'cause he's sure to give me credit — he's known me for a long time — about those façades, so that our home will be attractive and neat... I'll prune the trees. I'll turn over the garden. I'll repaint the shutters...

She'll come to see how I'm getting along.

She'll come in the evening (he breaks out in a smile, all alone on his landing). I'll say to her, "You see, it's coming along..." She'll say, "Oh, yes, you've made a lot of progress..." And I'll say, "Tomorrow we start fixing up the bedrooms. What wallpaper should we put up? I told Paltani to bring over some samples..."

Let's see, he said to himself, if they give me six months, or eight months, when will I be free? He counts it up. That's fine. I'll still have three months of good weather ahead of me. Yes, July, August and September... I'll get the trees pruned and the vegetable plots turned. Everything will be finished in time for the grape harvest... These things take time. I'll also need enough time to prove that I know how to keep my word. But then she'll be there and the house'll be ready... What color, he says to himself, should I paint it? Pink or maybe blue, or even yellow or white?

For there are blue ones, yellow ones and pink ones hereabouts... I'll have to ask her... I'll tell Paltani to slap some samples on the side facing the village and then I'll say to Thérèse, "Do you want to come and take a look?" "Ah!" she'll say. "What's this?" "Well, it's so you can choose..." "Ah!" she'll say. "It's pretty, why can't we paint the house in all four colors?" "That's fine with me, but what will people say?" This amuses him on his landing.

He lights another cigar on his landing. In the semi-darkness here, he lights a brand-new cigar and sees a great light rising over his life. That's what freedom is. A woman and a house of one's own. The mountains, they're beautiful, but they have no love for you... They are bright and white in the air before you, but they neither see nor listen to you. They don't look after you. There are thousands, thousands and thousands, of them — and you, facing them, you are all alone...

He passes his hand over his cheek. He says to himself, "That's not all. I also need to make myself presentable."

He had to light the lantern in order to shave himself.

XV

There was a gendarme pacing back and forth in front of the post office, and one at each end of the street.

Joséphine had to take precautions. Crittin was out of sorts. Crittin was anxious and in a bad mood. Seeing her as she went out that evening, he said to Joséphine, "Where are you going?" In reply, she made a gesture with her head to convey to him that she couldn't tell him in front of the patrons. He let it drop. She left the drinking room. She then races up the two flights of stairs to her room. There, she sees that her suitcase is too heavy and will be a hindrance. She says to herself, "Too bad!" She opens it and pulls out a skirt, a blouse and a shirt; she rolls them all up together to form a round bundle she can carry under her arm. If someone asks me where I'm going, I'll say that I'm taking some washing to a friend, or I'll just drop the bundle before anyone sees it. People can be heard talking in the drinking room, but she managed to get down the stairs without attracting attention. She reached the garden. She acted as though she were going to hang out some laundry to dry. Unwinding the clothesline from one tree to another, she made her way little by little down to the wall at the foot of the garden. But apparently no one noticed her, as she was separated from the gendarmes by the full height of the houses. As a result, she reaches the wall and now she is concealed by some currant bushes. All she had to do was climb over the wall. The masonry is old. The masonry is full of cracks and holes where the mortar has fallen out. A few steps more, then she says to herself, "Farewell, gendarmes." She too knows the paths, even the most secret ones; she knows them all, both the ones he told her about and those he didn't. This time, she'll come by way of the gorge and surprise him, but she has to hurry, for the other two entrances might well be being guarded, if the gendarmes know about them, or at the very least kept under surveillance from a distance. I'm going in the way we'll be leaving. This time he'll have to come. She clambers through the brush up this high, stony slope that drops sheer towards the valley floor. Cautiously thrusting her head forward between the bushes at the top, she looked again to see whether the exit from the tunnel was being guarded. It is just below her, this exit, which forms a black hole in the light-colored rock. Through it flows the water of an irrigation canal (what the people call a *bisse*), which joins the mountain stream higher up, at the bottom of the gorge. She sees that the exit isn't guarded, just as she thought. Ah! Those gendarmes don't know the passages the way he does, or I do, that's to our advantage — meanwhile, she drops down the slope from one projection in the rock to the next — and now Farinet will have no choice but to follow me. She arrives at the *bisse*. Night is coming; it is dark and the stars are appearing in the sky. All of a sudden, they have disappeared. Now it was darker than the night for her, much darker than the darkest night, as she advances like a blind person, with her eyes wide open and leaning her hand against the hewn rock wall. Fortunately, along the whole length of the *bisse* there ran a path used for making repairs. It is a tunnel about fifty meters long, and so low that she has to duck her head and bend forward, but the rock wall is there by her side faithfully the whole way. She merely has to follow it, pressing herself up against it as much as possible, which she does, while the water on the other side of her rushes straight along almost without a sound, because it is deep and the incline is quite even. Finally, there appears before her a kind of arched window the color of lead, yet almost bright in comparison with the shadows around it. This is the exit, that is to say, the entrance. This is the entrance to the high gorge, where she suddenly found herself in a grayish half-darkness where the rock walls are dark brown, high, straight and parallel. If she raises her head, she sees the stars again up there, seemingly arranged in a line, due to the narrowness of the space they are in. When she lowers her head, her gaze drops, drops some more, drops ever deeper towards something she can't see, something that whispers and circulates there. Now she can clearly see, up above and in front of her, the spot where the cave entrance is. A few fir trees reach as far down as the entrance, which is concealed by the branches of a bush hanging in front of it. She knows what to do, because he showed her where she has to leave the *bisse* and how she can make her way, from one projection to the next, bit by bit up the rock wall — something they don't know, yes, them, those men in their uniforms, with their képis and their stripes made of wool or metal.

"Tô!"

She called out the first time while climbing up and there was no reply. But suddenly she can see that he is there, because a faint light is coming through the branches.

Ah! He's there; he hasn't left yet; all is well! She calls out a second time. She calls out louder, now that she can risk it.

She steps onto a projection of the rock and, grasping a root (with the bundle under her other arm), she comes closer.

"Tô! … Tô! …"

She saw that he moved towards the entrance to the cave, thanks to a shadow projected against the middle of the disk of light, which is now quite close.

Does he hear? She doesn't know; she keeps on calling.

Then she comes out with, "Ah, what luck! I was afraid you'd already left. I have everything we need. I have the bank-notes…"

Then she heard a voice saying, "Is that you there?"

"Yes, it's me."

"What's going on?"

She still couldn't see him, or at any rate not well, since she was off to one side of the cave entrance. She came to a stop.

"You have to come quick, Farinet, hurry up…"

She can hear that he is calm, just a little surprised, because he said, "Come where?"

"Come with me. We have just enough time. They're on their way here. They're everywhere."

"Who is?"

"The gendarmes."

"Aha!"

Then there was a silence in which Joséphine could hear the nails in her shoes creaking. Then he was there before her. The storm lantern reveals that he is clean-shaven and dressed in his Sunday best, with a clean shirt, a collar and a tie.

"Well, aren't you handsome?" she said. "Where are you off to?"

Then she understood, and she started to laugh.

"So it's all over, Farinet… Ah! That's right, you don't know, do you?"

She looks at him steadily.

"You don't know, that's right, you don't know a thing… Well, it's like this: someone has robbed the postal clerk… Yes, someone took her banknotes and replaced them with some coins, *your* coins… And you don't know who pulled it off, do you, Farinet? No, that's right, you don't know a thing, living down in your hole."

He can't think of anything to say.

"You don't know? Well, it's me…"

Then she lowers her voice.

"Farinet… You said we didn't have any money… Farinet… It's so we'd have some, some real money…You understand?"

She calls out to him, because he seems not to hear her.

"Farinet! ... Farinet, I have the banknotes right now..."

She touches her chest.

"Farinet, yes, eight hundred francs ..."

At that, he shook his head and said, "Too bad."

"Why do you say 'too bad'?"

He sighs. Once more he said, "Too bad."

"Oh, Farinet..."

And letting her bundle fall, she took him by the arm.

"Are you coming?"

"No."

At that, her tone of voice changed. She asked a second time, "Are you coming? No, you don't want to?"

A third time, she asks, "You don't want to?"

XVI

NOTICE

So far, all he could read was this word in the title. It was written in pretty, rounded letters at the top of a large sheet of paper covered with writing, but he couldn't read anything more. All he could read was the title, and old man Bruchet had come and read it.

He hardly slept anymore, being too old and too racked with rheumatism.

He had scarcely closed his eyes when he was woken up by a pain in his shoulder or in his leg, or in his hand or his back. That's why he lit his lamp, but he could see that it wasn't three o'clock yet, so he put it out, then he relit it because he was bored lying in bed.

And he had gotten dressed quickly, for he hardly ever got undressed anymore. He had opened his door; it was five o'clock in the morning. Everyone was still asleep, but he sees — living, as he does, opposite the official notice board — he sees this sheet of paper that wasn't there the evening before. All he had to do was take his cane and hobble across the street.

Then the light increased a little bit; it flared in starts, as when one raises the wick on a lamp. Behind the old grille on the front of the wooden case, which hung in front of the communal hall, he saw the paper grow whiter and the print grow darker as these two colors separated from each other.

He read:

NOTICE

Now he sees, next to the title, the coat of arms of Valais with its field of stars, while here and there along the street, which was still choked with brown dust, he also sees some windows lighting up.

He is leaning on his cane; he has plenty of time.

NOTICE

And look — with a new spurt of light, the wick of the day was raised a little more.

Whereas our gen-dar-me-rie is on the trail in pursuit of Farinet, sentenced to nine months ...

Aha! Then he hears a key turning in a lock and the sound of footsteps on a staircase, but he continues reading, word by word:

...of imprisonment for making counterfeit coins, the authorities and citizens are called upon to provide assistance to our agents whenever and wherever required...

He hears someone asking him, "What is that, Father Bruchet?"

"Come take a look," he said.

And there were two of them in the pretty, pink light, each one reading from his own angle.

"Aha," said the new arrival. "Ah, well, they've started to shake a leg."

He too is reading:

NOTICE

and he too sees the coat of arms of the State with its eleven[13] stars, then:

We hereby order the communal authorities to deploy, night and day, until further notice, the personnel necessary to guard the vicinity of their commune and the bridges leading to it, with orders to arrest Farinet wherever he may be found and to hand him over to our police ...

"Have you read it?"

And the man points at the sentence, while another person says, "And then what?"

Now there are five or six of them. The newcomer says, "Haven't you heard? They've arrested Crittin."

"No, really?"

"Yes, last evening, just as he was closing up his café... Not only that, they turned the place upside down. That's how they found his gold."

"You don't say!"

They are all talking at once. Only old man Bruchet keeps silent, because he reads less quickly and less easily than they do.

...The use of firearms is authorized only in the event of resistance... The Government has resolved to put on trial, showing no leniency, any individual accused of violating Article 416 of the Criminal Code, to wit: "Those harboring, or causing to be harbored, persons known by them to have been sentenced to imprisonment shall be punished with detention for up to six months or with a fine of up to 300 francs...

"Hey, this is no joke!"

"And what about this?"

For the notice went on:

Any person who, by speech or otherwise, takes Farinet's part, whether in a public place or in the presence of police officers, or under any other circumstances, shall likewise be considered to be in violation of the aforesaid article and brought before the courts...

At that, they say nothing more to one another and look around themselves mistrustfully, because people are coming from all directions — women and children, along with two gendarmes. The men had just enough time to read the final sentence, which ran:

The Government has resolved to increase to 300 francs the reward to be granted to the person or persons helping to bring about Farinet's arrest.

From up there, through the telescope, he couldn't see any-thing at first but a white disk with gray hairs like those on a patch of mold. He has to slide one tube into the other one carefully in order to adjust the telescope to his eyesight.

"Oh, what do you see, oh!" said Pierre. "Pass it to me."

"No," said Félicien, "it's my turn. You'll get yours in a moment."

The two of them were up there, that is to say, at the very edge of the pasture, on the top of the escarpment that plunges straight down to the plain. The herd was about to go back down; the preparations for departure were already underway.

The well-polished, brass tubes gleamed in the light of the newly risen sun.

Once more, they had below them the whole valley, filled with mist that rose as if from a vat of boiling water — an immense, oval vat, as deep as it was wide.

"What do you see, Félicien?"

"Hold on!"

An immense vat yawned wide open below them. They were lying on their stomachs side by side in the curly grass.

Leaning on his elbows, Félicien moved his right arm back-ward while holding the telescope in front of his eye with his left hand. To make sure that the telescope was in focus, he aimed it at one thing, then at another. He was in no rush.

"Hurry up!"

Now Félicien hands the telescope to Pierre.

"I don't see anything. Here, it's your turn."

This was on account of the rising vapors. Some were spread in broad layers over the slopes; others, grayer and more transparent, were stretched out flat, between you and the plain, and blocked the view.

"Uh-huh, that's right," said Pierre. "You're giving it to me because there's nothing to see. And when you can see again..."

But at this very moment, a light air from the north started to blow from behind you and chilled your ears, then it slid down the slope and caught the mist from underneath. It was like a lever, or even more like a gravedigger's spade used to turn over a clump of sod. All of a sudden, you saw the clouds of mist rise swiftly in front of you, then, carried southward, slide over the top of the range. Now the village came into view down below you. To the naked eye, it appeared to have been dusted off, like a room swept clean with a feather duster. You could see the valley floor with its colors restored — its green meadows, its yellowish stubble-fields, its woodlots, its bushes looking like grass, its roads like white threads. Meanwhile, there was the Rhône, like another road, grayer, wider, more temperamental, hemmed in by its banks of immobile sand — another road, this one in motion.

"Hey!" said Pierre suddenly. "I can see some of them."

"Whereabouts?"

"One," said Pierre, "one, two, three, four..."

Holding his telescope pointed down to the east of the village, beyond the gorge, he counted.

"And then five, six... and two more..."

"Oh, let me borrow it, please, just for a moment..."

"But give it right back to me...There, you see..."

Félicien has to adjust the tubes again. Then, in the disk of light at the end, he sees a stretch of road come into view between a stony embankment and a small vineyard. Then, on the road, these black dots spring to life; they're not much bigger than flies, but they shine, throwing off flashes of white.

This was the visor of a *képi* or the frizzen of a musket or the handle of a yataghan. Indeed, there are eight gendarmes, counted off in turn by Félicien. This is to the east of the village, but there is also the valley floor, more to the south, where the road comes in from the capital.

They both counted, one after the other. Here, there were ten of them — ten gendarmes coming, in double file.

They were a little bit in front of Mièges and to the south, on the flat, bare road. Thus, in the end, the two contingents will reach the village from two sides, so as to take up positions at both ends of the gorge.

"They're sure to cross the bridge in Chiésaz," said Pierre.

"Then the others will head down below the village," replied Félicien. "That's what they call a maneuver. Ah, poor Farinet!"

But Pierre retorted, "Aw, they'll never get him."

"You don't think so?"

"Not on your life! He's much too clever and quick on his feet. I'm sure he'll show up at our place, just like last time."

He has the telescope again and he scans below with it, his head peeking over the edge of the rock wall, beneath the beautiful sky and in the bright sunshine. But there is no one on the path. Now Pierre passes the telescope to Félicien. Then he pulls his handkerchief from his pocket and unties it; the coin is in one corner.

He has brought it out into the sunlight, where it shines. He said to Félicien, "Do you have yours?"

Félicien nodded his head.

"Well," Pierre went on, "if he comes back here, he's sure to give us another one, don't you think? ..."

But he was interrupted by Félicien, who said, "Look! What's that?"

And, down there on the plain, behind the gendarmes, three little black dots were coming up. Two of them are shining, but the one in the middle isn't.

"You know what?" said Félicien. "It's a woman."

"A woman?"

"Yes, you can't see the daylight underneath…"

It was indeed a woman. It was Joséphine.

In the middle of the night, the man on guard duty at the gendarmerie barracks in Sion had been awakened with a start, for he was asleep with his elbows on the table. He raised his head with an effort and half opened his eyes, which were still bleary with sleep. He was saying to himself, "What is that?" Then he said to himself, "Is someone knocking?"

And, in fact, there was someone knocking. The knocking began again, this time harder, at the glazed door with a curtain of grayish cloth hanging in front of it.

At first, she was so out of breath that she couldn't speak, after running for more than two hours. The gendarme kept asking her, "What's the matter?"

Leaning against the door frame, she merely kept opening her mouth wide.

"C'mon now, what's the matter?"

At that, she said, "Come quick!"

Then she said, "Farinet… come… I'll show you… Come quick… the path…the exits…"

So the alarm was raised in the barracks, and they went to get the commander, who questioned her. Then, when morning came, they put her aboard the first train, along with one of the contingents.

All of a sudden, she started to talk, after saying nothing for a long time. (Meanwhile, the vineyards glide slowly past on her right; in those days, the trains didn't go very fast yet, because the line had been in service only a short time and the train stopped at all the stations.)

She was alone in the compartment with the sergeant and another gendarme. Suddenly she looked at the sergeant, and perhaps it was because he was old, with a gray moustache, she said, "Sir... officer, sir..."

Seated next to him, she had lifted her head. A vineyard passes by, its poles visible between the yellowing leaves and the clusters of grapes turning brown.

"Oh, I'm not what you think. I'm sure you even knew my father, because you're the right age..."

Here is what she said.

"Pellanda," she said. "Pellanda, Joseph...That's why I'm called Joséphine. He was a stonemason... We're Italians, but that doesn't matter. People have the right to be Italians... He came here as a little boy, to carry mortar... But," she said, "what are they going to do to Farinet, my God, sir?..."

The sergeant made no reply, simply nodding his head from time to time, by way of showing that he was listening all the same. Encouraged by this, she talked, she went on talking.

"You know, that's the common practice... The Italian workers would hire a kid to carry the mortar. They would cross the Simplon or the Great Saint Bernard in the snow... My father often told me about it... But you must have known him, sir, and my mother, too, needless to say... Because she was from these parts, she was a Zufferey...And my father never went back to Italy, needless to say. Never, never from the age of thirteen to the day he died ..."

The sergeant nodded his head; the train whistles. Then the thunder awakes beneath its wheels, because they are crossing the Rhône.

They made her get off the train. She walked along, held by the arm on both sides; she had fallen silent again. She walked along and, to make her stop, they merely had to yank on her manacles; if she stopped on her own, they just yanked them in the opposite direction. Long before she arrived in Mièges, the villagers caught sight of her from the windows of their homes. She was pointed out well ahead of time, when she was still down there on the plain. To get a better look, the people had come out of the village and gathered in groups along the wall that bordered the road. The two boys with the telescope are up at the top of the escarpment; lower down, in front of Romailler's house, stood Romailler and the dairy master, who had stopped by to say hello.

It was then that Romailler said, "It's all so sad. I don't understand any of it... He was supposed to come and give me his answer last evening. He left me a message saying he would..."

Romailler shook his head and went on, "And things aren't going so well around here, either. I don't know what's gotten into the girl... She looks terrible, she's crying. She didn't want to get up this morning..."

And the master said, "Are you coming? I'd like to go and see what's happening..."

Romailler declined.

And all this time she was coming, she was getting closer and closer. They all kept as quiet as they could, on account of the six months in prison that the notice threatened you with. They pointed it out to one another with a head movement. At this hour, it blazed white behind its rusty grille:

NOTICE

Any person who, by speech or otherwise, takes Farinet's part[14] ...

It blazed white at this hour, all white, behind its rusty grille. They pointed it out to one another as they walked past.

And as for her—she was approaching, she and the two gendarmes. The villagers saw her as she came, walking between the two. They were going fast, in step, extending their legs together, right leg, left leg, not slowing down despite the upslope. Standing at the entrance to the street, the people saw her, forced to come along as fast as the officers. The sergeant held the end of one of the chains in his left hand; the other gendarme held the end of the other chain in his right hand. Her hands hung down, but they were pulled up whenever she slowed her pace. She was red, covered with dust, her blouse half unbuttoned, her neck bare, one of her braids undone and dangling down her cheek—and all at once she saw us and wanted to stop, but she was immediately tugged forward.

"Ah, the Judas..."

This was Fontana.

Most of the people had, moreover, already taken the precaution of moving away from the street, and had gone inside the front halls of the houses or ducked behind a half-closed door. Scarcely the only ones left were two or three women and old man Bruchet with his cane. Old man Bruchet spat on the ground three times, the moment she passed by.

One woman crosses herself.

Another woman gathers her little girl against her body and hides the girl's face beneath her apron. *She* goes past; she said nothing and walked with her head down. She arrived in front of Crittin's café, which had remained closed. She seemed not to notice it; she didn't even raise her head.

And the people wondered, "Where are they taking her?" For she had crossed the village (which, to tell the truth, can be crossed in no time), and having crossed it, she hadn't stopped, which meant that the gendarmes had continued on their way. Then the people began to show themselves again. They emerge from the houses or descend the lane again. They set out to follow, keeping their distance.

"Ah, the slut, where's she going?"

But they found out soon enough, when they reached the end of the street.

From there, the view extended over the whole area to that side of the village, all the way to the gorge and beyond.

It extended over all of this ground, bereft of dwellings and half cultivated, with a few vineyards and no trees, then Farinet's house in its abandoned garden and, lower down, the tower in ruins. She was still moving along, between the gendarmes.

They saw that a guard post had been established midway between Farinet's house and the tower.

They saw that that was where she was being taken.

The commander, Monsieur de Sépibus, came out in person to meet her. It was at this moment that a voice was heard, saying, "Hey! Don't you see? On the tower…"

Someone had appeared at the top of the tower. This someone turned towards us. He raises his arm.

This arm is holding a white handkerchief; then this arm is waved in our direction as a sign to us.

It was him; he was bidding us farewell.

Farinet said farewell three times. At that same moment, she stopped short.

"Move along," said the sergeant.

And he tugged on her manacles, but she reared back and struggled.

"It's not him…" she said.

We understood perfectly well what she was saying, since she wasn't that far away.

"It's not him… It's not him who stole… It's me… No, I don't want to go… This is unjust! … No, I won't show you…"

143

Then we felt the earth move beneath our feet.

A white column, such as when one gently blows pipe smoke from one's mouth, rose next to the tower, from which some stones fell, while other, smaller ones flew straight up into the air. Then we received the explosion like a punch to the chest.

It was Farinet setting off his first mine.

The second went off right afterward, causing the house to collapse, sagging to the ground like a balloon deflated with the prick of a pin.

And the roof that had been above the tree branches was now below them.

He said farewell to *us*, but first he had gone to say farewell to *her*.

How he managed to leave his cave, that night after Joséphine's visit, is something no one ever found out. However, he had succeeded in getting out. It was not to escape. He had something else to do. If he had wanted to escape, he could have done so. That was not his intention. He simply left his den, then went back. He went to say farewell to Thérèse. For a long while after Joséphine's departure, he had remained seated close to the storm lantern hanging on the wall. He didn't stir, in his Sunday finery, and from time to time he shook his head beneath his new hat. He shook his head and his close-shaved cheeks; again he was in no hurry, again he had time. First of all, he needs to see that what he had thought possible is impossible. For a long time, he shakes his head in this manner, then he straightens it up and stares in front of him, in the soft and feeble light of the lantern, which creates a hazy disk in the air, as the moon does when bad weather is in the offing. What does he see? He sees something. He sees that it can't be. He took his notebook from his pocket, a notebook with a waxed cloth cover and an elastic band. He writes something on a blank page that he tears out and folds in half. He hasn't changed his clothes; there's no longer any point. He goes calmly to the lantern, which he takes in his hand, then moves forward, stooping, into the passage leading to the ladder. But a little before reaching the ladder, he swung to the right and entered a second passage. It had a lower ceiling than the other one, and was less well maintained, but Farinet merely had to duck down with his shoulder turned sideways, his neck outstretched and his arm extended. Meanwhile, the dim light in his hand quivered like that of a miner's lamp. Since the other exit had to be under surveillance, he chose this one as a precaution, on the assumption that it wouldn't also be guarded. Still, he just had to check to be sure. This he did. He came at last to an old wooden door, half rotted, which was latched shut. He listens. There is not a sound. Carefully, he drew the latch. Still hearing no sound, he opens the door. Then there appeared to be a second one in front of him, but on closer inspection, one could see that it was the rear end of a barrel shoved against the wall. He merely had to move it aside. Then he listened again for a long while. There was no one around. He reckoned that there must not be enough gendarmes yet to man all the posts. All the same, he had to look sharp. He had to pay attention for another moment longer, to keep from getting caught. After that, there would be no further need to do so.

Instead of his rifle, he has a six-shot pistol, late model, tucked into his belt. He comes out into the open again. He comes out, one last time, into the light of the stars, like a faint dust around him on the tops of the leaves, as he crawls beneath the bushes. Then he arrived in the vineyards. Here he paused for a moment. He saw a patrol pass by just below him. It is headed towards the gorge and forms a black spot against the blue landscape. He merely had to keep still for a brief moment. He is able to go over things in his mind again. "It's better this way," he says to himself. "Better for both of them." He thinks about the one, then about the other. I would have made them suffer needlessly.

"She's a good girl, Joséphine, I don't hold it against her. She's a good girl, a bit jealous, but quite devoted." He set out again. "And if Romailler had given his consent... No," he said to himself again, "I didn't have the right... Thérèse doesn't know what life is like... I was born in the wilds; I'm going to die in the wilds."

He sees that he is now no more than a few paces away from Romailler's house. Everything is quiet; there is no need to hurry. Once again, he sat down in the fresh air, in the damp grass behind a bush... "It's better this way. I won't turn myself in and they won't take me alive... That's the truth of it," he said to himself. "That's what I'm going to do" — as he looks one more time all around him.

Beneath the dark sky, the mountains were indistinctly white. They were suspended in the air like delicate lacework, floating midway up in the sky, due to the way their somber bases merged with the darkness. I'm not turning myself in, I'm remaining free like you until the very end. He is speaking to the mountains.

From the north and from the southwest, towards Vaud, towards the Jura, to the north, to the south, to the right, to the left, once again they are all there, as he can see: the Italian ones, the German ones and those with names in our sweet language, la Pointe à Pierre, la Becca Nera, in the language of our home. Well, then, to the very end with you (he is speaking to the mountains). That's the truth. Such as you made me, to the very end (this is what he is saying). They thought they would have me in their *galleys* again. They won't. It's better this way. Farewell, then, Thérèse, because I have come to bid you farewell. Farewell to you, mountains. And then I will say farewell to you, too, little one, but not right away. He feels his hands getting damp in the grass, and it is good. And so farewell, first of all, to you mountains, the ones I know and the ones I don't know: the Italian ones, Monte Leone way over there, and then you German ones (with his eyes he traces the peaks of this delicate, gray lacery, with a hint of blue in places, as when one has bleached the linens), the Cervin, the Dent d'Hérens, the Dent Blanche, the Grand Cornier. Those whose names one learns in one's mother's womb — the sweet, good, maternal mountains that one knows so well: the Colon, the Pigne d'Arolla, the Ruinette (one more time); the Combins, the Vélan, the Jorasses, Mont Dolent. Next, there is a valley whose crease in the mountain range is so well marked that it is plainly visible — a deep, long valley ending in what looks like a pocket full of crystals, the way all those Aiguilles are jammed together there: the Verte, the Rouge, the Argentière, the Dru, the Tour (and this is home). He says, "This is home." He says farewell. It's the site of his village. Then he takes a brief moment to go back again in thought: that's where the high pass is, with the dogs and the monks and a little lake — hey, farewell! — with patches of snow along the edge of the lake year round, with the tall gray house and its sheet-metal roof. But faithful to you to the very end, he thinks, and so farewell. And in a little, windowless house, the dead are lined up, standing or seated against the wall, in their habits, and there is one who is holding his head in his lap.

Faithful to you to the very end, mountains, and to freedom. He goes on: then comes the Tour Saillère and the Dents du Midi, and other peaks farther back — in Savoy or the Dauphiné — farewell, then, to the whole earth, farewell to the countries of the earth. Meanwhile, he gazes at all of them one more time — and the sky is dark, the stars white, and around him nothing stirs.

The time has come. He sees that the time has come. He removes his shoes.

He stands up. He has done everything quietly, making sure with his hand that his pistol is still tucked into his belt. Don't make a sound, he thinks to himself.

Let her not hear me, if she is asleep; let her not hear me, even if she is awake. I have only come to bid her farewell.

CHARLES FERDINAND RAMUZ

He seeks a spot where he can slip between the bushes without making any noise.

He takes the notebook from his pocket. He removes the sheet that he tore out and folded in half. Then he stoops down and chooses a large stone. Holding the stone in one hand and the sheet in the other, he stands at the fence.

He didn't want to push the gate, for fear of making it creak. He climbed over the fence. He sees that the shutters on the second floor are shut tight. He sees that those of the bedroom above — her room — are, on the contrary, only half closed. First, he mounted a few steps without making a sound. Then, clinging to the wall and placing his foot on the cornice, he bends down.

He places the sheet of paper on the windowsill and the stone on top of the paper.

I only wanted to bid you farewell.

Then he climbed back down the wall without making a sound. She heard nothing.

XVII

By morning, the gorge had been completely surrounded. De Sépibus, the commander, had positioned guards at each of the exits and every place where Farinet might have had the slightest chance of escaping. Then he had Joséphine brought in for another round of questioning.

There were about ten of them, seated around a large table in the meeting room of the communal hall. Besides Commander de Sépibus, there was the mayor, the four councilmen including Romailler, the communal clerk, and Madam Rey with her son. Meanwhile, the side of the table nearest the door was unoccupied.

Now she appeared and stood there, with a gendarme on her right and another one on her left. Her hands, on account of the manacles, were a bit separated from her body. And before M. de Sépibus even had a chance to begin speaking, she said, "No, it isn't him... And this is unjust, because it isn't him, it's me ..."

"Be quiet!" said M. de Sépibus.

"No," she said, "no..."

She had forgotten that her hands were bound. She tried to raise them, then she made a noise like that of a goat in a hedgerow when it shakes its bell in a frenzy.

"Be quiet!... You'd do better to tell us how you managed to get into the post office...if you really are the one, as you persist in claiming..."

"Yes, it is me."

"Be quiet... Madame Rey..."

"Oh, that's right," said Joséphine. "Madame Rey will be able to tell you. About how she locked up the street entrance, but not the one from the garden. Because I'm the one,

I assure you. He's innocent... I swear to you he's innocent... There's a storage room on the ground floor, isn't there? Do you think I didn't know about it? And the window had a broken pane. Isn't that true, Madame Rey? You see, Mister Commander? All I had to do was come and open the window. And once I'm in the room, there's a door that connects to the office, isn't that so, Madame Rey? And the key to the drawer, Madame Rey, you know very well where you've been hiding it, and so do I... Yes, in the corner of the writing desk, that's where, under some old documents and account books..."

Madame Rey nodded, since everyone was looking at her. It should be noted that she was much calmer, now that they had recovered her eight hundred francs.

"Well, then, Mister Commander, you see, it was just a matter of taking the key and opening the drawer. I took the banknotes and left the coins in place of them... It isn't him, it's me. Oh, what was I thinking? And what are you going to do to *him?* Oh, don't do anything to him. He's innocent, I tell you. I wanted to force him to come with me, because he didn't want to leave. He said he didn't have any money. Me, I said to myself, 'If he has money, he'll come.' But he refused to come..."

Again she made a movement with her hands, which were not altogether immobilized; again they heard the jingling of the chains, as she turned to face Baptiste Rey.

"This is all your fault..."

"Mine?"

"Yes, yours."

He ventured to say, "Why?"

"Ah, maybe you don't remember... Yes, you, when you came..."

"Be quiet!"

Baptiste was turning quite pale. But Commander de Sépibus intervened again.

"Be quiet!"

She obeyed. For a brief moment at least, she obeyed and fell silent.

"So you maintain that you're the one? Clerk, take it down… That you're the one who committed the theft in question…"

"Oh, yes, sir. Oh, yes, I'm the one, and he hasn't done a thing… So, sir…"

Her tone of voice changed.

"And don't do anything to *him*. You won't, will you? As for me, I've already been punished more than enough. It makes you jealous, you know…"

Romailler and the mayor hung their heads. The interrogation went on. Then they took her away. Madame Rey and her son left to go home.

Once they were alone, the gentlemen began a discussion.

"Maybe this isn't quite fair," said Romailler. "It wouldn't do to push him over the edge."

"Gentlemen, we are faced with two crimes: defiance of authority and theft… Even supposing that Farinet is not guilty of the latter, which I am inclined to believe, he is no less subject to prosecution for the former."

Monsieur de Sépibus was a well-spoken man.

"That doesn't take into account," he went on, "the counterfeiting…"

"That's true," said Romailler, "but he isn't a bad fellow…"

"And," said M. de Sépibus, who had been ordered to arrest Farinet, dead or alive, "it is all the more important that I accomplish my mission, because large contingents of gendarmes have been mobilized. This kind of operation can't be mounted twice."

"However," said the mayor…"Couldn't we? … It's just that the people are attached to him, you know…"

It should be stated that there was considerable discontent in the commune. Since no one dared talk about these things in public, they took refuge in the stables behind half-closed doors. They kept their voices low that morning. "What should we do?" Fontana was there, as was Ardèvaz. They all said, "We should go and rescue him."

"There should be two or three of us," said Fontana.

"What about the guards?"

All the guard posts were occupied, that is to say, all the exits from the gorge — the tunnel, even the bed of the stream. He was trapped like a mouse.

"And what about her?" someone said. "Where is she?"

"Oh, she's locked up in the communal hall."

"If I had her here," said Fontana, "I'd strangle her."

They talked low in the cowshed,[15] which was still vacant because only one animal was kept around during the summer, for milk, while the others hadn't come back down from the mountains yet — one animal that was bedded down at this time and peacefully chewing its cud, absorbed in its own affairs. And aren't we likewise absorbed in our own? However, they couldn't come up with any solution.

Just when the only thing they could think of was to go and talk to the mayor, they saw him heading up to his house with Romailler.

They learned then that Romailler had obtained permission from M. de Sépibus to go and talk to Farinet before they issued the final warning.

So Romailler, with his hands cupped around his mouth, leaned over the opening to the cave, which had to be about twenty meters lower down. He couldn't see it, for the plunging rock wall formed a kind of overhang.

"Farinet, this is Romailler… Romailler from the council… I have a message to give you…"

He fell silent. At that, the echoes, alert and ever quick to have some fun, emerged from their hiding places, with bursts of speech, with laughter and whisperings, which lasted a long time and drowned out the sound of the water.

The echoes had heard, but had he?

"Oh!" said M. de Sépibus, "if he doesn't hear, it's because he doesn't want to."

He was there with the gentlemen of the law and three gendarmes, one of whom had a bugle. He went on to say, "But keep it short and space your words out, if you want him to understand you."

"Farinet…"

Nothing.

"Do you hear me?" Romailler went on.

Nothing.

"I'm here to tell you… Joséphine Pellanda… She's confessed… We know."

Nothing.

"So, Farinet… I came to tell you…They'll take it into account…You have to surrender…"

The echoes came again: "render… render… ender…" Then they died away, and the noise of the water could be heard again.

And it was only after some time had passed that there came a voice, and this voice said, "No."

It said "no" calmly; it spoke softly. They were surprised that it came from so close by — the lengthy silence had led them to believe he was either absent or quite far away. Farinet was right there, no doubt sitting at the entrance to his cave. He spoke to them as if from the corner of the hearth, with no need to raise his voice.

"No."

Romailler looked at the commander, who shrugged.

But Romailler steels himself for another try.

"What do you want to do, Farinet? ... If you don't turn yourself in...you'll be taken... Farinet, think of your friends... You have them, you know... Everyone likes you... They'll be happy to see you again... I'm here on their behalf..."

Once again came the reply, "No."

"You see," said M. de Sépibus. "It's useless."

"Yet I have to try again... Farinet, hey! Farinet..."

"No."

The men were waiting for Romailler at the entrance to the village, because he had forbidden them to come any closer. From the distance, they saw Romailler shaking his head in discouragement. At the same moment, they heard the bugle — it was the legal warning.

One might have thought that the gendarmes were about to attack immediately, because their deployment alone cost the State an enormous sum. But they knew that Farinet was well armed and that he was surely determined to defend himself. In this, he had a great advantage, because the passages were narrow and numerical superiority meant nothing there, for only one person at a time could enter them. Hence, the attack had still not taken place when, during the afternoon, a man presented himself who was from Lignerolles, a village nearby.

"Is there a reward?" he said. "How much is it? Well, then, let me do it... It's in my line."

He was a chamois hunter, or so he said.

"And I don't know him personally myself. I've never dealt with him. Besides, I won't hurt him. Do you have any ropes?"

They went in search of them.

The man already had a plan. He said, "You need to send some men to the other side of the gorge. They'll shoot at him. That'll make him keep his head down."

He was a short, lean man, with a brown goatee, who seemed to know his business and cared little what others thought, for he said, "After all, he's an outlaw."

He was armed with two late-model six-shooters, like Farinet's. They tied the rope around his waist according to his instructions. And he repeated, "It's three hundred francs, right?"

"Three hundred."

"For me?"

"Yes, if you get him."

"Well, then, let's go."

Two gendarmes descended a few meters to the first fir tree, around which they wound the rope. This was on the second day, in the afternoon.

The people came out of the village again. They crept closer and closer, gathering in groups, men and women, brimming with anger and saying, "What's he butting in for? He's not even from the commune. We'll smash his skull." Though barred for now from intervening, they were nevertheless driven by curiosity, with the result that two gendarmes were assigned to keep them at a distance.

Meanwhile, the set of ropes was being put in place. Then a patrol was dispatched to the other side of the gorge. They were three men, who were barely visible, having immediately concealed themselves, spaced well apart from one another, behind clusters of boulders. The man with the goatee began his descent. He went about his task and seemed to know what he was doing. The rock face was neither absolutely vertical, nor featureless. On the contrary, it was full of projections, recesses and, as it were, hitches, which made for an easier descent, but slower going. The man searched for a handhold; having found it, he signaled to the gendarmes to pay out some rope, which they did. The rope could be seen waving and twisting for a moment like a grass snake. Free to move again, the man stretched out one leg, then the other one. It all took place amidst a profound silence and nothing stirred anywhere — the people thought that the gendarmes posted on the opposite side of the gorge must have spooked Farinet. The man descended. The rope, which had grown taut again, went slack once more. Midway along the pitch, there was a small fir tree where the man regained his footing. He signaled again for them to loosen the rope, and they paid out a meter or two, but it probably hindered him when it happened to draw up too tight. At this, he signaled for more rope, the gendarmes up above following each of his gestures with their eyes. Visible just below him was the bush that concealed the entrance to the cave, then nothing more but a gray and indistinct shadow, at the bottom of which rushed the mountain stream.

Thus, they had paid out the rope as the man had instructed, four or five meters in all. It was at this moment, when the rope was still quite slack, that they heard the sound of something sliding, while stones tumbled down.

Then a great laugh went up and a voice came (the noise of the stones having barely ceased after their vault into the void).

"Ah, so much for that... Ah, you thought... You thought it would be so easy... Maybe you thought I didn't know a thing..."

And the laughter immediately reached the village, where the people knew right away what had happened.

"The bastard fell! Serves him right."

Fortunately, the rope held the man back just as he came to the bush, but he had to be injured.

Farinet's voice came anew.

"Just come down and get him."

They couldn't see Farinet. He was speaking from below the bush, in the depths.

"You just have to come down. I'm not at war with traitors or clumsy fools."

The man was whimpering, "Ow! Ow!" Then he said, "Hey, up there, I can't move anymore. I'm pretty sure I have a broken leg." They saw that his face was covered with blood as well.

Two gendarmes had to descend, while others held the rope tight. Farinet hadn't budged.

"How many of you are there up there? Me," he said, "I'm all alone..."

It was necessary to fetch a ladder to bring the man up. He, Farinet, was just below them, and didn't interfere.

"Everything all right?"

He laughed. He said, "I'm sorry I can't come and help you," while the man complained loudly, because they had to haul him up bodily.

"Come again? If I wanted to... I could shoot all of you down without even showing myself. If they think they can stop me, the ones across the way, they're wrong. I have all the cover I need, and I don't think they have much of a view... Go ahead, just take a shot..."

And he held his hat out at arm's length.

A shot rings out.

"Missed!"

A second shot.

"Missed!"

"Take it easy," said the man. "Watch out for my leg!" The operation took a good two hours and it was getting dark by the time they finished.

The man was taken to the infirmary in Saxon. The night was calm.

XVIII

But, the next morning, he went over to his round loaf of bread. He saw that there was just a small piece of crust left, which he ate.

Passing his hand over the shelf of rock where he stored his provisions, he sees that there is nothing left but a few remnants: the cheese, the dried meat, the pears — for Joséphine had not come back and would never come back again.

For lack of kerosene, the lamp had gone out in the early hours of the night.

Now it was morning again. This was the morning of the third day. He came to sit at the entrance to the cave, his pistol in his belt and the two rifles ready to hand.

He said to himself, "This is the end." He said to himself, "All is well."

From where he was, he couldn't see anyone yet. He himself could be seen only with difficulty, due to the recess in the rock and the overhanging branches. But his supply of dry wood was also coming to an end. Nevertheless, he had lit the fire and he kept it going. From time to time, he rose to go and toss a handful of bark or some dry branches onto the embers, so that a wisp of blue smoke could be seen rising against the wall of the gorge.

That's to tell them that I'm alive — to tell them that I'm expecting them.

He still couldn't see anyone. There was still nothing but the rustling of the mountain stream deep down below. When he raised his eyes, there was the other stream overhead where the clouds, gilded and white, tore themselves apart, one from within the other, allowing tatters of blue to appear in their ragged holes.

That was all.

But suddenly a bugle sounded a two-note signal once. It falls silent. "Aha!" he said to himself. Then a second time, a third. He takes up one of his rifles; he discharges it into the air.

That's my way of answering them.

"For," he said, "I will be faithful to you to the end, stones of the earth, and to you, great rocks" — as he surveys them once more from bottom to top and scales their heights with his eyes. "O, mountain bedrock! We'll stay together to the end. Hey, you out there, are you coming? ..."

He began to talk out loud, without stirring from his place.

"Or if you're going start that business with the ropes and ladders all over again, like a bunch of acrobats, you're not up to the job and it isn't working..."

He was talking out loud, making a speech.

"How many of you are there? I'm all alone here... Hey, there! How many of you are there? At least thirty, with a commander, lieutenants, sergeants and corporals. Me, I'm all alone — that is, there are two of us, because I have freedom with me..."

Now they could hear him from the guard post just above him, where there were several gentlemen in civilian clothes (for more of them had come that day than the evening before), and there were five gendarmes.

"Because there's such a thing as freedom, and you have her on your medals and your coins, but I have her here in person and she is sitting by my side. A living, breathing freedom."

This was precisely the moment when the operations were about to begin, for they couldn't wait any longer. Above Farinet, they were getting ready to descend and renew the maneuver from the previous day, but this time armed with plenty of explosive devices. He fires a second rifle shot into the air.

"That's to warn you that I'm ready," he said. "You have bugles, I don't. You play the bugle. Me, I fire a shot with my rifle."

Then he carried on with his speech.

"On your diplomas, on your certificates of marksmanship, on your banknotes, your holiday cards — but it's just a drawing of a person. She's in a nightdress and barefoot; she holds a crown out to you, but she is counterfeit. Meanwhile, there is the true one, the one who is with me…"

And they listened, up above him, as they waited for the signal. They could understand what he was saying perfectly well, because he kept raising his voice more and more.

"…In the air and in the clouds. With me, by my side and sitting on the stone… You're too late," he went on. "She'd left me for a time; she's come back. She said to me, 'Farinet, what did you have in mind? …' I said to her, 'You're right, you're all I have.'"

He was interrupted by a new bugle call, then pebbles began to tumble down, passing through the air in front of him and disappearing, in utter silence, into the void.

He fires another shot with the rifle.

"Your freedom, what is it? Hah! Imprisoned the way you are! Hah! Given a number! Freedom is written on your walls, but just look at what's underneath… They're called regulations, decrees, laws, permits — they're called authorizations. Me, I'm *authorized* to die."

At that, in various places around the gorge, a multitude of stones began to fall.

"You don't know who I am! The king of Italy didn't know, either… And you — you thought you could keep me in your *galleys*. I didn't stay there long! Now come and get me! …"

He stood up; a gunshot rings out. He raises his hat above his head.

"Missed!" he shouted.

He begins again.

"Bid Joséphine adieu for me. Tell her I don't hold any grudge against her. She's a good girl!"

A gunshot.

"And also tell everyone that my gold is good, that…"

A gunshot. He then went out onto the ledge, provoking them to fire at him from all sides.

"That it's true, that it's good, even the truest and best of all…"

The fusillade had ceased, and they could hear Farinet quite well, but they could no longer see him.

He must have gone into one of the vertical creases that plunged, at lengthy intervals, down the face of the rock, splitting it from top to bottom. From there, he yelled, "Decanted pure from the living rock!"

At that, a loud voice, coming from who knew where in the midst of the rocks, interrupted him.

"That's true!"

And Farinet said, "You hear that, you men from Sion, you gentlemen of the law, you gendarmes?…"

Then someone shouted, "Farinet, stay where you are. We'll come, two or three of us…"

"Like the most beautiful wine," said Farinet, "once it's settled…"

"Stay put, Farinet…we're coming."

And no one ever found out who spoke this way, who or

how many they were, or where they were, since they must have hidden themselves somewhere among the rocks.

"The color of harvest time…the color of *her* hair…"

The shooting suddenly commenced again, drowning out his voice. He had left the ledge he had been following up to that point. From one projection to another, he lowered himself down the rock wall. Then someone shouted again, "Farinet, we'll come. You should just give yourself up…"

"Never!"

They continued firing at him.

He took off his hat and waved it over his head once again.

"Missed!"

Then he continues his descent, and they couldn't see him anymore. Then they saw him again.

He had started out onto another ledge that slanted down-ward, but here he came face to face with some gendarmes who had been posted at this end of the gorge.

There came a volley.

XIX

Bong!… Why are they ringing the bell? The people listen for a moment; the bell has ceased. (This is when one strikes hard with the clapper against the inside of the bronze skirt, and the strong beat is at the beginning of the peal, which is then allowed to die away for a long time in the distance, like an overloaded cart jolting along…)

Bong!… Then they understood — it is the knell. But for whom are they ringing it? … You don't know? It's for Farinet. Do you remember the beautiful tureen he gave me for my wedding two years ago? …

Bong!… And six silver spoons for me… Well, they just found him. He hadn't come right away. He came along very slowly. Ah! That's because the water isn't swift, it's too deep, too black, and then there are places where it's dead still. So they had to wait… My God! …

Bong!… Those waterlogged clothes make it swell up and become heavy. It comes along, it stops, it gets stuck for a bit in the current of the *bisse*, it spins around for a moment, it disappears; it comes to the surface again; it turns and comes feet first…

Bong!… He's crazy, that Vacheret, to ring that way… Oh, he's got it into his head and won't let go. "It's not a suicide," he says… He's right. Tough luck for the authorities… And the gendarmes just had to wait, you see, then they fished him out with their rifle butts…

Bong!… Oh, you see, you see over there — they're coming, they've laid him on a stretcher. There's one gendarme at his head and another one at his feet… Yes, they've come to borrow a blanket and a sheet… And you see, just now they placed him inside the sheet and wrapped the blanket around him.

Bong!... He makes a hump with his feet at this end, and a smaller hump with his head at the other one... They're coming, oh, they're having a hard time of it. It's not easy, what with that path there — it's not much of a path, through those stones. You see, they're stopping already... Ah! How peaceful he is! You can see how he's not putting up a fight.

Bong!... So gentle he looks, turned all gray, so innocent and obliging... Oh, why? What did he ever do to them? And they were thirty against one! Why? He was always good to us. Do you remember (there were three of us girls; it was the Feast of the Patron Saint) the coins he gave us? One for each of us. Ah, he was generous...

Bong!... And good! A lad of our mountains. And tall!... *"The cadaver measured one meter seventy-five,"* read the coroner's report afterward... And strong! *"The appearance of the body offered the picture of a vigorous man with a good constitution in the prime of life, who appeared to be between 25 and 30 years old. His hair was blond; he bore a small red moustache ..."*

Bong!... And handsome! *"The nose was straight and sharp, the eyes blue and the forehead high and prominent..."* Ah, what have they done to him — one of us, a lad of the mountains, a hunter, a boon companion...

For the whole village had turned out to meet him as he was carried uphill. There was indeed a gendarme at his head and a gendarme at his feet. He came, tucked up well beneath his blanket. The gentlemen of the law were there waiting for him. Us, we spread ourselves out in groups more towards the back.

He came on, just a little bit above the ground. He had to be terribly mangled; fortunately, we couldn't see anything. *"He bore a few slight scratches on the nose and the face, a transverse wound about an inch across on the right temple… The parietal and frontal bones were crushed…*[16] *The stomach was flat and empty, containing only a few crumbs of bread…"*

This is what they read later in the coroner's report, at which Romailler shook his head. "Ah! The poor wretch!" And the mayor said, "Ah! The poor wretch!"

He passed before us. Meanwhile, there was one person, up there in the white house, who went to close her window in an attempt to hear no more, yet she hears nevertheless. Then she jams her fingers in her ears and hides her head in her hands.

Bong!…

Ah! Yet he was good, handsome, tall, strong, generous, easy-going—you remember—a lad of our mountains! And he passed before us. The gendarmes followed with their rifles, and these gentlemen of the law fell in behind them. Us, we brought up the rear, while the knell kept tolling.

Ah, just let it toll… It's one death, a poor death, after all… Like us, one day, and like these gentlemen… yes, like these gentlemen, when it's their turn—in spite of their fine clothes, their sabers, their sword belts and their bandoliers…

At this moment, we saw the bailiff come running up the street.

†

"Have you heard? She hanged herself."

"Who did?"

"Joséphine."

They were speaking in low voices.

"Where?"

"In the prison… She hanged herself with the cord from her apron…"

The knell had just fallen silent when the gendarmes arrived in front of the communal hall.

Someone said, "She heard the bell ringing; she understood… She made a slip knot with her cord and passed it around her neck. She attached the other end of the cord to one of the bars. And then she kicked over her chair…"

†

[1] *Liberté* is a feminine noun, as is *lune* in the next paragraph. Ramuz vividly personifies both "freedom" and the "moon" in this scene, hence my use of the personal pronoun "she" in place of "it" to refer to them. See also Farinet's last speech in Chapter 18, where the personification of "freedom" is made even more explicit.

[2] *Chalet*, in this context, denotes something quite different from what the term has come to mean in present-day English. Rather than an accommodation for tourists, it refers to a cabin used seasonally by shepherds while tending their flocks high in the Alps. The first definition of chalet provided in the *Trésor de la langue française informatisé ("Digital Treasury of the French Language")* reads: "Alpine cabin, in which shepherds take shelter during the summer and make cheeses." (My translation — JW) The definition is accompanied by a citation from Ramuz's novel, *Derborence*.

[3] Literally, the sentence begins, "He laughed in his beard," for which the usual idiomatic equivalent in English is, "He laughed up his sleeve," i.e., covertly. However, Ramuz keeps pointedly referring in this scene to the master's beard. The intention is clearly to emphasize the word "beard" as being somehow expressive of the master's authority and cunning. Hence, I have retained the somewhat awkward phrasing.

[4] Ethyl alcohol. An archaic term in Parisian French, but according to Ramuz still current at the time in Swiss French. See note 3 to this chapter in the Pléiade edition, *Romans, vol. 2 (Gallimard, 2005), p. 1637*.

[5] For the use of the feminine animate pronoun, see *note 1* above.

[6] Their laughter is not prompted merely by Joséphine's confusion. The men recognize an allusion in Farinet's questions to the climactic scene in Charles Perrault's fairy tale, "Blue Beard," familiar to every French-speaking person. Blue Beard's wife, fearing death at his hands, hopes that her brothers will arrive in time to save her. She asks her sister to go to the top of a tower and watch for their appearance. As Ramuz uses it in *Farinet*, the wife's rescue at the end of the fairy tale is steeped in irony.

Her sister Anne went up to the top of the tower, and the poor afflicted wife cried out from time to time, "Anne, sister Anne, do you see anyone coming?"

And sister Anne said, "I see nothing but a cloud of dust in the sun, and the green grass."

In the meanwhile Blue Beard, holding a great saber in his hand, cried out as loud as he could bawl to his wife, "Come down instantly, or I shall come up to you."

"One moment longer, if you please," said his wife; and then she cried out very softly, "Anne, sister Anne, do you see anybody coming?"

And sister Anne answered, "I see nothing but a cloud of dust in the sun, and the green grass."

"Come down quickly," cried Blue Beard, "or I will come up to you."

"I am coming," answered his wife; and then she cried, "Anne, sister Anne, do you not see anyone coming?"

"I see," replied sister Anne, "a great cloud of dust approaching us."

"Are they my brothers?"

"Alas, no my dear sister, I see a flock of sheep."

"Will you not come down?" cried Blue Beard.

"One moment longer," said his wife, and then she cried out, "Anne, sister Anne, do you see nobody coming?"

"I see," said she, "two horsemen, but they are still a great way off."

"God be praised," replied the poor wife joyfully. "They are my brothers. I will make them a sign, as well as I can for them to make haste."

[Source: Andrew Lang, The Blue Fairy Book (London: Longmans, Green, and Company, ca. 1889), pp. 290-295. Accessible online at https://www.pitt.edu/~dash/perrault03.html]

[7] *Il y a de la chèvre par chez vous?* "In all likelihood, the reference here is to the chamois or alpine ibex, but this sense is not found in any of the dictionaries consulted." *Romans*, Pléiade edition, vol. 2, p. 1638, note 1 to Chapter 10. (My translation — JW)

[8] Not quite what Ramuz wrote. Taken literally, the original text is implausible: *Et, ayant enduit le chiffon de graisse, il faisait aller son bras de haut en bas dans le canon.* "And, having dipped the rag in grease, he worked his arm up and down in the barrel." Perhaps Ramuz intended to replace "his arm" with "the ramrod" or simply "it" (referring to the rag), but never got around to revising the text.

[9]A play on words here. Ramuz literalizes the idiom, *refaire le monde*, "to solve the world's problems," "to change the world." Recall that in Chapter 4, the boy, Félicien, amused himself with a telescope similarly, "destroying the world and putting it back together again."

[10] The coat of arms of the Canton of Valais does not look like this. It bears three vertical rows of stars, but there is nothing resembling the "wavy, horizontal lines" representing the river Rhône. The only coat of arms remotely matching Ramuz's description is that of the Canton of Aargau, in the German-speaking region of Switzerland. It is divided vertically into two halves, the left one depicting three horizontal, wavy white lines against a black background. The right half displays three white stars in a triangular configuration against a blue background.

[11] The first two utterances in this paragraph of dialogue are slightly cryptic. According to Ramuz's punctuation, they must be attributed to Farinet, referring to himself in the third person. "You" in the second sentence is the formal *vous*, indicating that Farinet has already turned to address some unspecified person or persons other than Lavallaz, the "young man weeding his vines," who has just exchanged pleasantries with his surprise visitor using the familiar *toi [tu]*. This is one of many examples of the way Ramuz abruptly switches the point of view among the villagers, in order to convey their shared attitude towards Farinet. Theirs is a feeling of solidarity, despite their fundamental disagreement with him over the proper conduct of one's life.

[12] Ramuz once again invokes, none too subtly in this case, the opposition of montane heights and valley depths as an "objective correlative" of the ethical dilemma confronting Farinet.

[13] "There are thirteen stars on the coat of arms of Valais. They represent the thirteen districts composing the canton. This slip on Ramuz's part is corrected in the Grasset edition." *Romans*, vol. 2, note 1 to Chapter 16, p. 1639. (My translation — JW. See also endnote 10 above.)

[14] A minor oversight on Ramuz's part. Earlier, the notice read "individual," not "person." The slip is noted in *Romans*, vol. 2, note 3 to Chapter 16, p. 1639.

[15] The men are meeting in what is clearly a cowshed *(étable)*, though Ramuz refers to it as a stable *(écurie)* a few lines earlier. There is no obvious way to reconcile the discrepancy.

[16] *Les os du pariétal et du coronal étaient broyés...* In referring to the "coronal bone," Ramuz makes a slight error, as there is no such bone. There is, instead, a coronal suture, which joins the parietal and frontal bones.